EVERYWHERE
BUT HERE

DOUG INGOLD

Wolfenden

EVERYWHERE BUT HERE

Copyright © 2024 by Douglas A. Ingold

ISBN 978-0-9973513-7-8 (print)
ISBN 978-0-9973513-8-5 (e-book)

Library of Congress Control Number: 2024908634

Published by

Wolfenden

Arcata, California
wlfndn3@gmail.com
wolfendenpublishing.com

Cover, Layout & Design:
Robert Stedman Pte Ltd, Singapore

Printed in the USA

Other novels by
Doug Ingold

There Came A Contagion

Rosyland: A Novel in III Acts

SQUARE

The Henderson Memories

In the Big City

Short Stories

Short and Shorter

This Novel is dedicated to

YOU

EVERYWHERE
BUT HERE

EVERYWHERE BUT HERE

a novel

DOUG INGOLD

… the brief sum of life forbids
our opening any long account with hope;
night hems us in, and ghosts, and death's close
clay…

Horace, *Odes* Book 1, 4
Translated by Robert Lowell

CHAPTER ONE

SCHOOL OF THE ART INSTITUTE OF CHICAGO

April 2, 2022

My Dear Robert:

Imagine my consternation! I call the number we have for you and I get the voicemail of some woman with a Spanish accent. The emails I send bounce back. You have disappeared from social media, your website is defunct. The alumni organization has no clue. Even my snail-mail letter was returned with the terse and unsympathetic observation that your forwarding address has expired!

I reach out to everyone I know. I call our fellow classmates. I call artists, gallery owners. No one knows what work

Robert Turghoff is doing, or where he has gone, or even if he is still alive. Even the critics do not know and the critics know everything. Just ask them.

Then at long last I get a text from Gordie Silt who tells me that he and his wife recently ran into you in Sorrento, Italy. Sorrento? Italy? He claims that the three of you had lunch, that you are living in the shadow of Mount Vesuvius and painting. Painting "The Ancient Enemies," you told them, as if that makes any sense. And all he gave me is this sort-of address. So, here I am and I hope there are you.

Now, to the business at hand. We have received an application here at SAIC from a young woman who claims to know you. She says that you were her first teacher. She swears you were a "great inspiration" to her, and exclaims that she remembers "your graceful hands."

I grant that eighteen-year-old-would-be-artists of either gender can be a tad hyper- emotional but I have known you for many years, and while I have always enjoyed your company, Robert, I have never thought of you as particularly inspiring or your hands any more graceful than those of the average artist, or for that matter the average cab driver or grease monkey.

But histrionic emotionalism aside, it was her assertion that you had been her initial teacher that raised a bright flag for me. I remember how eager you have always been to mock artists such as myself who teach. The old "Those who can do and those who can't teach" sort of smear, which is absurd of course but I have always let it pass as Robert being Robert.

To compound the situation, the applicant does not give you as a reference, which is odd given how eager she is to admire you. The claim is further compounded by the fact that she lists a street address in Santa Rosa, California as her home. And Google tells me that Santa Rosa is two or more hours from the now-defunct California address we have for you. Are we to believe that you, an artist devoted to nonteaching, traveled hours to teach a student, or that the child-student somehow made this long trek over and over to receive instruction at your studio?

So, Robert, I suspect that this applicant is using your name falsely, and, if that is true, perhaps the quite impressive portfolio she provides is also a fabrication.

The final nail in the coffin, so to speak, is found in the portfolio itself. As an example of her early work the applicant includes a drawing that she claims to have made as a twelve-year-old of a drawing you had made of her mother. Well, here was something on which I could hang my hat, because, as you know, the Institute displays in its museum three portraits that you made early in your career, one of which, I am proud to say, is a portrait of myself.

I have compared the submitted drawing closely with our proven examples of your portraiture work and I have concluded that the applicant may well be a skilled forger who intends to use a degree from our institution to further her nefarious schemes. Furthermore, given that you have disappeared from the art world, if not from the universe itself, what is to prevent a dishonest dealer from marketing the work of this woman over your name? After all, any third grader could scrawl TURGHOFF across a canvas with as much flair and more legibility than you.

So, that is the gist of my concerns about this applicant. I eagerly await your informed response.

On another note, we age, Robert, which, I assume, you have also noticed. When I revisited those three portraits our days together came back in a rush. Remember the dingy digs we shared in Hyde Park?

The second portrait, by the way, with its dark beard and black stocking cap is one you did of that buff, weightlifting sculptor you hung out with for a while. The one who killed himself driving drunk on the Dan Ryan. I forget his name, Sergei something. We used to call him the Black Russian, remember? Thank God he went out alone that night!

The third portrait, of course, is your sketch of the lovely Alicia Earls, who fancied herself a jeweler and was always polishing stones and bits of silver and twisting strips of copper into brooches and earrings, and whom I much fancied for myself. I recently had an opportunity to revisit Max Klinger's sculpture, "die Neue Salome." Do you know it? Such a haughty, naughty girl is this Salome done in stony marble with the severed heads of John the Baptist and Max Klinger himself at its base. Max had a taste for revenge all right, and seeing it brought the haughty Alicia to mind. Ever coy she was, drinking those endless cups of coffee from the same mug. I have never forgiven you for stealing her away from me. Don't know if you know, but I heard that after she got free of you she married a politician of all things.

Do you believe it has been a decade or more since we last saw each other? That small gallery off Superior…I forget the name, something French-ish I believe. It's closed now, shuttered and gone. The pandemic of course. A good crowd though for the opening night of your one-man show. You covered the walls with thorny canes, twisted vines, decaying leaves and other weird vegetative stuff. Seems all rather kitschy now, does it not?

So, "Ancient Enemies," is it now? Gordie Silt described the sample you showed him as "monstrous" and unlike any Turghoff he had ever seen. Sounds like madness to me. Come home, Robert! Come in from the cold! I can get you on as an instructor. Really! Painting, drawing, you name it. And tell me about that applicant. Is she friend or fraud?

Yours, Elwood

LONG BRANCH, CALIFORNIA
SIX YEARS EARLIER

CHAPTER TWO

One afternoon the painter Robert Turghoff went to see his friend Solomon, the chiropractor. Solomon had remodeled one of the old "mill" houses on Laurel Street for his office and Turghoff parked in front, killed the engine and then sat behind the wheel for a few moments to collect himself.

In the heady years following WWII when fifty or more sawmills were operating in the area and lumber trucks chased log trucks up and down the highway from dawn to dusk, most all the houses on Laurel Street were modest, wood-framed, single-bath homes. Over the years most of those houses had been expanded, or demolished, the small lots merged and larger homes constructed. But across the street from Solomon's office one of the original mill houses remained.

An elderly man named Jim Franklin lived in the house, and when he heard a vehicle pull up across the street, he looked away from the TV, leaned toward the window and peered through the blinds. The vehicle he saw that afternoon was an aged GMC pickup, greenish and well dented. As he watched, the driver's-side door opened and a man climbed out. About fifty, Franklin guessed, his skin rust-colored by the sun, muscular enough, but not tall. A "David Crosby" mustache curved over his upper lip and brownish, sun-lightened hair hung unkempt about his ears and curled against the base of his neck. The man wore sandals on his bare feet; a pair of baggy shorts approached his knees and a neck-stretched T-shirt covered his chest. The color of the shirt, like that of the shorts, had faded to a uniform irrelevance.

The man moved slowly as he extricated himself from the truck and approached Solomon's office. Franklin watched him pause at the door. He saw him balance himself, legs apart, and press his right hand against the wall and carefully pull the door open with his left. Then he disappeared inside.

Franklin had gone into the woods for the first time at the age of seventeen, following his father up a steep hill carrying cans of fuel and chain oil, and he had spent his working life harvesting timber, everything from hauling green chain to felling trees to bossing crews in a silver hardhat. Watching from the window, he knew well what the fellow's problem was. "Back trouble," he muttered as he turned again toward the TV.

§

Earlier that afternoon, swimming nude as usual, Turghoff had completed a few laps in his outdoor pool. When he emerged from the water he took the long-handled skimmer and rescued a drowning wasp he had spotted in the water. He was hanging the skimmer back on the brick wall when Montoya the plumber came through the gate. Montoya carried a cooler with a six pack of Coronas and was followed by Edgar, his twelve-year-old son. Montoya dropped onto a chaise lounge, opened a beer, and started to complain about Alita, his ex-wife. Alita had just told Montoya that Edgar needed more dental work and claimed that Montoya had to pay for it. As usual, Edgar was running around like a crazy person.

"That's why I pay child support," Montoya told Turghoff. "She says child support doesn't cover dental. Dental is extra, she says. She tells me to look at the papers. It's all in the papers. But I don't have the papers. I threw the papers away a long time ago. She knows that. That's why she can mess with me. She feeds the kid nothing but candy. Candy this, candy that. Then she wants me to pay the dental."

This was Montoya's idea of parenting, it seemed to Turghoff. You pick the kid up on a Friday afternoon. You bring him over to Turghoff's. You sit and drink beer and complain about your ex-wife while the kid threatens to destroy himself and everything around him. Turghoff did not begrudge Montoya's coming or his complaints. Montoya worked with sewage all day. He coaxed mechanical snakes down reluctant sewer lines; he stood in filth to wash out tanks, replace failing pumps, floats and switches. Things broke, slop spilled, everything smelled and Montoya made it right again so the rest of us could avoid smelling it, looking at it, or thinking about it. The man had every right to complain about whatever he wanted to complain about.

Turghoff called the kid "Headlong" because when he set off running he gave no thought to stopping. That, apparently, was what trees, walls and other people were for. Headlong had already kicked off his flip-flops. He had thrown his T-shirt and shorts on the cement apron. Now he was running full speed toward the pool and throwing himself at the water. Over and over. The idea seemed to be: make as big a splash as possible. Do belly flops. Do cannonballs. Yell like an insane person. The more chaos the better.

Turghoff thought that Montoya might be wrong about the dental, but right about the candy. He did not know Alita well but he remembered a voluptuous sense of entitlement: thick, with shimmering hair, awning-like eyelash extenders, plastic nails that extended the fingers an inch or more. She worked somewhere in school administration.

Headlong was a big kid for twelve, round, fleshy and hairless. Parts of him quivered like a bear when he moved, and he was always moving, a roaring, vibrating tornado made of stuff more deadly than wind and rain.

When Headlong was younger, eight or nine, Turghoff had made a mistake; he got into the habit of wrestling with the little tyke. In the pool, on the lawn. He would roll him around.

Pick him up and heave him into the water. Slap his ass, his head and shoulders. Show him wrestling holds he remembered from TV. The little kid had loved it, and he still did, but he was no longer a little kid.

So Headlong was remembering this scene from a movie he had seen on TV. Going on and on about it. Begging Turghoff to do the scene with him. The good guy is standing beside a pool, see, and a bad guy rushes toward him. The good guy turns around just in time. He grabs the bad guy and throws him over his shoulder and into the water. Turghoff could be the good guy, and he, Headlong, would be the bad guy. "I come running.... Okay? Okay?" Insistent as a jackhammer. So Turghoff had finally agreed to try it one time. "Just one time, Headlong, that's it."

And now, as Jim Franklin had observed, Turghoff was headed for the office of his friend Solomon, the chiropractor.

CHAPTER THREE

It was August, not Turghoff's favorite time of year. In the part of northern California where he had made his home for the past quarter century, August was the cruelest month. T.S. Eliot had been wrong about April. Out here April was packed with bluster and promise, with new leaves filled with light and splashes of sudden snow. Even dark December, the month everyone loved to hate with its short days, its low gray skies, with storms pushing in from the Pacific, with power outages, and rivers swelling beyond the warning stage and threatening to flood, with slides of mud and rock moving relentlessly across roads, even December gave you something. It enclosed you and yours within a cocoon of hardy shared survival. It energized. It bolstered. It turned you into a braggart of hardship: "Had an inch overnight." "Yeah? We recorded an inch and a quarter." And as his mother used to say on the solstice, that simple woman with her peasant's wisdom: Now the days will start to grow longer.

But August spoke to him of stagnation and faded promise. The grasses he loved, the wild oat, the sturdy timothies, their colors faded, their seeds flung, their heads wispy and tattered, their time spent. The fennel had grown spangly and started to seed. The hemlock looked beaten, finished for the season. Even the Queen Anne's Lace, that beautiful globular flower, had begun to curl itself into fists, its stalks gone purple. Smells dried up. A gray dust covered what green remained. The air turned hazy, the earth parched—no rain since mid-May. And those intense sunsets, the only vibrant colors to be found, were false. Tainted by smoke from wildfires near at hand or hundreds of miles away, August sunsets were distortions of true color, betrayals of true beauty like badly computer-enhanced photographs. Turghoff's father had died in August, and he assumed that some dry August his time would come as well.

He slowly pulled open the front door of Solomon's office. To the woman behind the desk he said: "Well, it's the Boss."

Patty, Solomon's wife, frowned. She did not appreciate the title Turghoff had bestowed on her, though in his mind it was true beyond question. Solomon had the license but Patty scheduled the appointments. She collected and deposited the payments. She paid the bills and planned their vacations and organized their weekends and handed Solomon his weekly allotment of pocket change. Who, pray tell, was assisting whom in this operation?

"He's with someone," Patty said.

In a community where dressing up meant putting on your best black hoodie, the one that on its backside listed the venues of some famous band's world tour that had taken place seven years earlier, Patty was as usual heeled and hosed, her face made up like a story, her earrings all a dangle. The emerald of her blouse, he noticed, matched perfectly the color of her eyes.

"I'm early?" he asked, surprised.

Another frown, as if the possibility that Turghoff could have arrived early was painful to contemplate.

"He's running late."

Then you and I will just have to sit and ignore one another, he thought. He lowered himself carefully onto the couch and was reaching for one of the several wine magazines neatly displayed on the coffee table when he realized that Patty was not ignoring him at all. Rather, she had removed her hands from the keyboard; she had joined them together in a prayer-like fashion and was placing them before her on the desk. She leaned toward him and cleared her throat as if his touching the wine magazines threatened her sense of decorum. But no, it was not that. Patty intended to speak.

"Robert, Yvonne has shared with me…some things."

Turghoff found this comment unpleasant in multiple ways. First, he was rarely called Robert by anyone anymore and the sound of his regrettable first name pronounced with such precise emphasis on the consonants evoked memories of grade school teachers, and the memories were not pleasant to contemplate. Second, the word "shared" used in this faddish way annoyed him. Intimacies were "shared" these days and wines and foods were "paired" and both turned his stomach. Third, and finally, Yvonne had mentioned that she and Patty were friends, but the news that she had chosen to confide in Patty was not welcome.

He decided to adopt the Churchillian strategy: never complain, never explain. He looked at Patty and said nothing.

"Yvonne has a daughter...."

Turghoff nodded. Yes, he was aware that Yvonne had a daughter.

"Carly is the same age as Britt, our daughter."

Turghoff had not known that, or at least had not thought about that, but he nodded his head again anyway.

"They are both twelve, you know, that age, and classmates last year at Sunset School. Patti Robinson's class. P A T T I, spelled that way...."

All of this was coming out slowly. It needed to come out; at least in Patty's mind it seemed necessary that it come out. But it was not easy, and seeing her struggle, Turghoff remembered that he and Patty Solomon went back a long way. Back before she was a Solomon. Back when she first arrived on this far edge of the continent from somewhere south of Hadrian's Wall, her accent then decidedly more British Isles than it was now.

She had been working her way slowly around the world, and Jen, that would be Turghoff's second wife and the mother of his two children, had met her in Way Natural, the natural foods store. One of those quirky things that happen, the two of them chatting in a checkout line, and Jen had brought her home for dinner and Patty had ended up living in their guest room for three or four months and caring for Marta, their own daughter who at that time was less than a year old.

Then one day Jen had suggested, with that scheming matchmaker glint she had, that they should fix Patty up with Solomon. Solomon was himself relatively new to town back then. He got by doing odd carpentry work: garden sheds, wood sheds, generator sheds, unpermitted slap-together projects including stretchers and frames for Turghoff's canvases. And now Solomon was a chiropractor working as his wife Patty's faithful assistant, and Jen was in a lesbian relationship with a gynecologist and was herself a surgical nurse a thousand or more miles away in Colorado Springs, and Marta was about to start her first year of college at Boulder.

Must be eighteen or more years ago now, but a clear picture arose of Patty at the dinner table that first night. A clever young woman with a mischievous sense of humor, her wide mouth, her greenish eyes, her thin neck, her slightly curled shoulders, her hair dark and frizzy beneath the tartan tam she had worn constantly when she first arrived.

He had done a portrait of her in that hat. He had not been satisfied with the mouth, he remembered, but the fabric of the hat, the colors and the texture in the tam he had felt good about.

Patty was still struggling. Leaning forward on the desk, her face a portrait of earnest intent, she seemed incapable of actually expressing her most pressing concern.

"And a husband," Turghoff offered now to relieve Patty's strain. "Yvonne, I understand, has both, a daughter and a husband."

"Yes," Patty said with cautious relief. "Yes, she does."

CHAPTER FOUR

The mural idea had come to Turghoff in a dream: a series of
large outdoor murals in prominent locations. He explained its
origin as a dream, though he did not remember the dream itself.
But he had woken with the idea vibrant in his head, as if it
were a shapely mushroom found fully formed on a path one
damp morning that had not been there the night before. It was
not so much that he came up with this idea, he told people, or
that he owned it. It was more that the idea owned him. The
idea appeared and it was saying, do this. And so for the next
several weeks the mural idea traveled with him. It informed the
way he looked at Long Branch, his small northern California
town, its buildings, its traffic patterns. It nudged his reading in
compatible directions.

    The town's energy was ebbing, everybody knew that.
The timber industry was long gone and the remaining protected

redwood groves had become passé. Commercial fishing on the coast had shrunk to nothing. The tourist trade had disappeared, and the seventies' flush of back-to-the-landers had gone flat. Those eager young hippies with their creative energy had become tired, cynical, gray-haired pot growers, and their children had fled to colleges or prisons or to urban centers far distant. Even the pot business, almost legal now, had been corrupted by the influx of Mexican and Bulgarian cartels creating huge grows, environmental degradation and violent crime—and the selling price had collapsed.

Empty storefronts were common now along Main Street. Meth-heads twitched in vacant doorways or slumped on curbs. The few tourists who did venture off the bypass and into the downtown, took one look around, gathered up their children and quickly returned to their cars.

After weeks of pondering the mural idea, and after mentioning it to a few friends, Turghoff had gone to a meeting of the local Chamber of Commerce where he rashly and clumsily introduced the concept. Murals in public places, he said, would add interest to the downtown while highlighting the area's history. He would design and compose the images but he wanted to involve students in the actual painting. The good old boys on the chamber board looked at him without expression. Then one of them asked about money.

"Money? Well, yes, money would be needed, and of course I expect to be paid for my time and expertise."

You, paid?

"I am a professional," Turghoff insisted. "I get paid for my work." Then in a moment that struck him as wildly inspired, he blurted out: "But not with public funds! With a very public fund drive."

Yes, that was the idea. The more involvement the better Turghoff told them: schools, kids, service clubs, the chamber itself, the county historical society. There might even be grant money for this kind of thing. The idea was to invest the town in its own re-imaging. Create a new identity, a brand if you will, one that would revitalize the community itself and at the same time tempt travelers off the highway to linger and spend their cash.

The chamber board thanked him for coming but the members looked dubious, glancing at each other like suspicious sheep. But the next day Turghoff got a call. A woman said she wanted to interview him. Mel Kline had told her to call. Turghoff knew Mel Kline. Mel was the editor of the *Weekly Register*, or as it was known by locals, *The Woeful*. But the woman was not someone Turghoff knew, or whose name he recognized from a byline: Yvonne Curtiss. On the phone she had introduced herself as: "Yvonne, double n, Curtiss, double s."

The woman who arrived at the studio behind his house the next afternoon was in her late thirties or early forties. She wore dark glasses and had dressed entirely in black. Her hair thick and black, flats black, slacks black, her blouse a pattern-less black. Both the slacks and the top were well styled and made of fine fabric. The blouse had a jaunty collar and an open eye-catching neckline. The juxtaposition stunned him. The woman who stood before him appeared both carefully hidden and brutally exposed. As he watched she removed a notebook and pen from her large black purse. A silver chain surrounded her right ankle. Three silver bracelets of varying thicknesses encircled her left wrist. Silver rings glinted from several fingers and still more silver protruded from the lobes of her ears. Around her neck two delicate silver chains hung to near her navel and on the end of one of the chains there dangled a small silver key. A key.

Turghoff was transfixed by the key. He believed in images and symbols. He believed in the fundamental reality of both. For Turghoff, form was substance and substance did not exist independent of form. And symbols? Well, symbols pervaded everything. And here was a key hanging from a delicate chain around this mysterious woman's neck.

He shook her hand and immediately began to think about how he might persuade her to sit for a portrait. He began by offering her a tour of the studio. But she seemed more interested in the building itself than the artwork hanging from the walls or stacked against them.

"If I told you what I paid for this place the first time you would accuse me of stealing."

"The first time?"

Yes, Turghoff was rather proud that he had purchased the property three times in twenty-five years. He and his first wife acquired it from the administrator of an estate. Then Wife One divorced him and he bought out her interest. That price was doable, he explained, because their equity at the time had been small.

"But the third time, the purchase from Wife Two, the mother of my children...we had almost retired the mortgage. So, it was like starting over."

"Another mortgage?"

"A whopper."

"Are you still paying?"

Turghoff nodded, pointing her toward some sketches hanging on the back wall. "My hope is with the money from the murals, I'll own the place free and clear. It must be a fine feeling to own your home free and clear."

He then realized that the woman was not looking at him or at the sketches. She was busy scribbling in her notebook. This woman was a reporter, he remembered. He should be careful.

"That was off the record."

"What was off the record?"

"That quip about doing the murals to pay off my mortgage. It wasn't a lie. I intend to get paid for the project, but my fee is a small part of the vision. We live in the midst of a rich history. People have occupied this land for hundreds of years, thousands, really. We know there was a native community along the river, if not year-round then certainly during the summer and fall. I have found arrowheads and other stonework in the ground outside this studio. They grew oaks for the acorns. Or tended them at least. Set the hillsides on fire to keep the conifers at bay. Did you know that? Big Hill out there is all redwood and fir now, but back then the near side was oak, if you can believe it.

"Then the first white settlers began to arrive. Farmers, ranchers, the logging boom, carloads of tourists in the fifties, roadside attractions. In the late sixties and seventies the hippies started moving in, city kids going 'back to the land.' Now they're the gray guys and gals walking around town. Influx and change. Booms and busts, tensions and times of cooperation. Chinese laborers passed through here when the rail line was constructed but we know precious little about any of that. Think what their lives must have been like! The conditions they worked under. Shortly after the war they put the bypass in. Before the bypass all that traffic came through town. Then there was the Indian massacre back in the 1880s. Seventy or more murdered, men, women and children. It happened just west of here in the cave above Indian Creek. The stories go on and on."

The notebook and pen were hanging loosely in the woman's hands. She had removed her sunglasses and was looking at the sketches.

"We can express this history in a series of murals," he continued somewhat desperately. "We can set ourselves apart from the other communities along the corridor. We can pull our young people out of their isolation and reintegrate them in a living community, a living historical context.... Are you getting any of this down? Anything other than I want to pay off my mortgage?"

"Most everything you said just now was in the presentation you made to the chamber. I have all that on tape," she said, still peering at the sketches.

"So, what are you doing here? You must have what you need for an article."

"I listened to the tape so I get the basic concept, the murals, the history, the kids, the community participation. That stuff, I know. What I don't have a grasp on yet is you. You are at the center of all this. The driving force, the creative thrust. Our readers are going to want to know about you."

"Fine. Ask away. I don't know how long you've been here but I am not an unknown in this community. Yes, I sell my work through outside galleries. Most of them in urban areas at some distance from here. So, I am not strictly a local artist, but I've had showings here. I'm part of the local visual arts community. Five or six of us had a weekly figure-drawing class for years. My son and daughter did some of their schooling here. And I've been connected to local political and environmental struggles. I've lived here a quarter century. To most of your readers I doubt that I am that unfamiliar."

"Nine months," she said.

"What?"

"I've lived here nine months."

"Okay."

"But this is about you, not me. And here's my point. Anyone can have an idea. Okay, you have an idea. Public murals highlighting the history of the area. Involve the kids, market the murals to tourists. Not a world-shaking idea. I doubt you are the first to have it. But that doesn't make it a bad idea. Didn't Edison say something about genius being ten percent inspiration and ninety-percent perspiration?"

"I think it was ninety-nine and one."

 "Whatever. But what's going to sell this idea? What has to transform the concept in your head to actual murals on walls is you, Turghoff. What has to be sold here is not just an idea, it's you. Who is going to take this idea and make it real? That's what readers want to know. Who is this guy?"

CHAPTER FIVE

As an artist and as an individual Robert Turghoff was a private person. He had friends, he socialized, but he lived alone and he worked alone. And the resulting art was his own. While some forms of artistic expression are inherently cooperative—such as staging live theater or movie production—others such as painting are more solitary and private. The whole point of being an artist, in Turghoff's mind, was the opportunity to bring into physical reality images that were personal and unique to his interior life: his interior life, his vision, his artistic expression. His favorite quote came from Georgia O'Keeffe: "I paint to express what I cannot say in words." Turghoff interpreted this to mean that O'Keeffe painted to express what she could not say even to herself. Filling a large canvas with a voluptuous black iris, O'Keeffe came to better know who she was. She became more fully Georgia O'Keeffe. It was this urge that formed and sustained him as an artist.

Of late the going had been slow. Economic downturns select artists as their first meal of choice, a tasty antipasto before moving on to meatier fare. To purchase a work of art is to express exuberance, a sense of wellbeing. Even the filthy rich pause briefly when the market plunges, as if everyone, the rich and the less rich alike, were walking in tight formation. Corporations hunker down. Museums clutch budgets to their chests. Marginal galleries shutter their doors and, if you are lucky, send back your pieces they had on display.

But Turghoff had seen these swings before. He felt he could intuit cyclical flows and he knew a bubble when he saw one. When the money flowed he spent it. When times were lean he tightened his belt. Buried beyond the woodpile out back were some quart-sized mason jars that he kept stuffed with twenties rolled and bound by rubber bands, the rolls packed in like dolmas, the lids tightly sealed. To ensure the reserves he needed, he grew a few marijuana plants every year. He trimmed his own weed and he sold it himself to artists and gallery people he had known for decades. Most everyone in the community played the same game to one degree or another. He never got greedy. He had no desire to be, or appear to be, extravagant. He was forty-nine now, but twenty-four when he and Alicia, his first wife, had purchased the property. He had been at this business for a quarter century.

He made the greater part of his living selling his art, though he liked to say he did not do art to make the living: he made the living so he could do the art. He had been trumpeting that wisdom for years, but the pronouncement had begun to sound a little hollow.

A sense of discomfort haunted him of late, and it was not just the economic downturn. He had accomplished the major goal of his life. He had made a successful career for himself through his creative output. As a student he had mocked his teachers at the Art Institute. Dilettante painters, he thought of them. They do their daring academic art while securely salaried by the institution. That life was not for him. No, he had come west with a sketchpad and a new wife. He brought his own vision, his own discipline, and he had fashioned a life and a career for himself. He owned a home and a studio. He had a reputation well earned; galleries wanted his work, buyers purchased it. He was not rich, he was not a celebrity, but he was known and admired for his work.

But having done what he had set out to accomplish, he felt now an emptiness. Another canvas completed, another painting sold. Thousands of miles away in some couple's fancy Bethesda home a piece of his was now on display. "It's a Turghoff," they tell their guests. Drinks in hand the wealthy folks study it. Well? Well, so what?

He was coming to feel a little jealous of people like Montoya. Perhaps plumbers, teachers, caregivers, were onto something. They served a greater good. What good really was his art doing in that swanky Bethesda pad?

Thus came the idea of the murals.

And with the murals he was tantalized first by the technical challenges. He had not previously produced a visual design that would be applied to an exterior surface. He would need to find an appropriate wall at an appropriate location. He must gain the approval of the wall's owner. And the image had to be acceptable both to the owner and to the community at large. He would have to prepare the surface properly, determine the appropriate paints (the sun fades some colors more quickly, he had been told), obtain the supplies and equipment including scaffolding, and then somehow project the design onto the surface, sketch it out and fill it in (rollers, sprayer, brushes?) and finally he would have to apply a sealant in some way that would preserve the finished image against the vagaries of sun and weather. (He decided early on that he would talk about a series of murals, thus giving himself a de facto ownership over the concept, but his focus was to create one successful mural.)

At times during his career, he had produced works of art on commission for corporate offices, creations that needed the approval of a board or an executive. But a public mural would require a far greater willingness to cooperate, to collaborate and compromise than he had previously imposed on himself. How then did one develop and preserve a personal vision while bringing it to fruition through a process as public as a mural? All of this challenged and excited him. It was this time of his life, he decided. *I am ready for it.*

CHAPTER SIX

"There is a rumor that you paint in the nude. Is this rumor true?"

In his studio that afternoon, Yvonne, double n, Curtiss, double s, sat in good light on a high stool before a white wall. And he stood a few feet away before a large pad of sketch paper set on an easel, a charcoal pencil in his hand.

She had removed her shoes and her right foot was perched parrot-like on the stool's bottom rung. The left foot lay across it, the front of the left ankle resting on the Achilles tendon of the right. Turghoff had studied anatomy and was fond of feet, which in this case were long and narrow.

What fascinated him was not the shape of the feet so much as the innocence of her gesture; the naiveté he found in the position her body had taken, the posture and poise. Had he full freedom on that afternoon he would have drawn only those feet, those ankles, one with its delicate silver chain, the way they perched there innocent, forgotten, stunningly real. Everything one might want to study was present in that composition of ankles and feet, it seemed to him: mass, tension, balance, support, elegance and decay: a hint of a bunion, a smudge of callus. All of it joined and suspended without plan or thought, as complex, as captivating as a skyscraper or a bridge.

But freedom is never full. He was a mural-man now, and this woman, he was coming to realize, was integral to his overall plan. And they were getting along well, it seemed to him.

"My readers will want to know, that's why I'm asking."

"I will not be nude when I paint the murals."

"Can I quote you on this?" He heard a low voice and murky mirth.

"The subject hardly seems apropos."

"Well, rumors abound and you will be working with children. But seriously, I have heard that. Is it true? Do you paint in the nude?"

"I have been known to paint nudes. Perhaps you misunderstood."

"No, my source—and I can never reveal my sources, even if sent to jail—my source was very clear. You, according to my source, are a nudist, and being a nudist you paint in the nude, weather permitting."

"Weather permitting."

"Yes, according to my source."

"If you look closely you will see that I am painting now and I am not nude."

"You are not painting now. You're drawing or sketching or whatever. But not painting."

"True."

The toes, what he could see of them, were tortured. The pinkies were pressed in and squished under as if cowering from the light. The long first toe on each foot seemed determined to curl over the toe adjoining it as if it were an arm flung in sleep over the shoulder of a bedmate, though in this case the impression was of torment rather than languor. Red-painted nails heightened the sense of anguish. Her claws had been clipped, stained and constrained. They were domesticated claws painted the color of blood to give the illusion of vitality. But the reality was more pained than vibrant. For whatever reason this woman had sentenced her feet, that most crucial portion of herself, to a lifetime's confinement in improper footwear. Thus the paradox before him: from knee to toe a flowing image of both grace and discomfort. On the one hand pain and angst and on the other elegance and innocence. And he was fascinated.

"Don't move!" he said abruptly, just as she was about to. "Not your feet, not nothing."

At the sound of his voice she jumped as if jolted by an electrical current. The strength of her reaction surprised him. She looked distressed.

"My feet? Don't do my feet! My feet are awful."

"Just don't move."

She groaned, but held her position as he continued to sketch.

"I used to do this on the street," he said, hoping to distract her. "In San Francisco years ago when Wife One and I moved west. We were kids. I would set up in that open area near the chocolate factory. You know, at the Wharf. Pen and ink. Twenty bucks a portrait. Alicia worked in a sandwich shop and she'd come out on breaks. We ate lunch on a bench and watched the people. Not a bad life, really, if the weather was decent."

"Robert, really," she said, "I need my purse."

"Which usually it wasn't. Alicia said later that she never enjoyed a single warm moment in San Francisco. And she was from Boston."

"I'm becoming very uncomfortable."

"Just a minute."

Turghoff believed that what he thought and felt as he was creating a work of art would find its way faithfully into the art he was creating. It was not necessary, in other words, to over analyze, but it was important to not be scattered or distracted. The channel between mind and hand had to be open and uncluttered so both were free to initiate and respond. He felt himself moving into that groove now. Thus he ignored her pleas and continued to sketch.

"Christ!" Yvonne jumped from the stool and ran to a table where she grabbed the large black purse. Her back was turned toward him, but he could hear the rattle of pills in a plastic container. Her hand went to her mouth and her head jerked back. She stood motionless for a moment, shoulders hunched, head forward; then she turned to face him.

CHAPTER SEVEN

"I have met the daughter," Turghoff said to Patty Solomon, still holding the wine magazine absently in his hand, "Carly, is it?"

"Yes, Carly."

"But not yet the husband. The kid seems pleasant enough. She came by the house with her mom. Yvonne had told her about a sketch I did of her that first day. The girl wanted to see it. Yvonne tells me Carly has an artistic bent. She wandered around the studio while her mother took some photos for that first article, the one about me promising not to paint murals in the nude."

"I read the article," Patty said, her expression unpleasant. "I suppose everyone did. That's why we keep paying to put ads in the paper. Solly has more than enough business. We don't need to advertise. But even with the online sites now, even if the printed news is a bit dated, everyone still reads *The Woeful* because it tells us who we are. It's a kind of conversation, I suppose. I always go first to the letters to the editor. Isn't that curious? All that hard news, accidents, drug busts, high school sports, obits, births, weddings, an editorial or two, and yet, I start with the letters."

"That was her idea, not mine," Turghoff said. "About the nudism. I would have preferred it not be mentioned. What's the point? It has nothing to do with anything the article was about. But she insisted."

"And a significant percentage of the letters are crank letters," Patty continued. "I don't read the crank letters. Not the real cranks, I mean. They'll publish anything. That's part of the charm, I guess. But I find it worthwhile to separate the real cranks from the sort-of-cranks. I read the name of the writer first and then decide if I'm going to read the letter. That one guy is still harping about getting the US out of the UN, can you believe it? Him I don't read. But the sort-of-cranks, I enjoy. The quirky ones."

"She's decided that if I want to sell the mural idea, I have to sell myself, nudist and all. The 'complete you' is how she put it."

"She may be right. She's turning you into a quirky crank. Everybody loves a quirky crank." Patty chuckled, pleased with herself. "But isn't there a distinction between a reporter and a press agent?"

"What do you mean? She's a reporter," Turghoff said.

"She started as a reporter but the impression I get is she's becoming your agent. A series of articles. She's already done two and more are coming. Isn't that the plan?"

"Her idea, not mine. Look, Patty, I believe in this project. Public murals. It can be a win for everyone. The kids, the business community, the whole town. What am I supposed to do? Call Mel Kline and say no more articles? That would be absurd. Yvonne thinks the project is a good idea. Kline agrees that a series of articles, so long as she keeps them fresh and interesting, would benefit the paper as well as the town. It creates a sort of ongoing narrative and something different from the usual DUI accident, hash lab explosion or meth-fueled murder. Everybody gains and nobody loses. I don't see the problem."

"She's vulnerable, Robert," Patty said quietly. "Yvonne is vulnerable. All three of them are. Carly is extremely vulnerable. She is a wonderfully sweet child. Britt loves her like a sister. We love her too, she's almost part of the family. But believe me, Carly is fragile."

Turghoff let that sink in for a moment. Then he explained to Patty that Yvonne wanted him to give the girl some lessons, drawing lessons.

"I've never done that before, not even with my own kids. I'm an artist, not a teacher. A teacher is a whole different thing. A profession to itself. What do you think?"

"Drawing lessons? Well…that could be a good thing, I suppose. For Carly. But I'm worried frankly about your deepening involvement with Yvonne. And now drawing lessons? Isn't that maybe just an excuse for the two of you to get together?"

Turghoff finally allowed the wine magazine to fall back onto the table. He placed his hand on his back and winced. The muscles along the left side of his spine were going into spasms again. He felt trapped. And there was nothing he hated more than being trapped.

"What is he doing in there anyway? Reconstructive surgery? Wasn't my appointment for four thirty?"

"Robert, you need to understand. This family...."

"What family?" Turghoff was twisting around on the couch like some drugged out contortionist. The spasms were in the middle of his back; he could not reach them from above or below.

"Yvonne's, of course."

"That family…"

"Gil…Yvonne's husband…there have been problems. I don't know what she's shared with you..."

There it was, that word again. Turghoff felt compelled to groan. Patty was watching him but he saw no signs of sympathy.

"There had been a separation in Santa Rosa," she continued. "Where they were before. Then they got back together. I think they really do love each other by the way, and they are good parents. They would do anything for Carly. So, they made a big decision. They would relocate. Get away from the stresses and the circle of friends where the problems were.

They came up here to start a new life. Gil got on right away with one of the propane distributors. Those blue trucks, he drives one of them. And now Yvonne's found this opportunity with the paper. They're trying, all three of them are really trying, but it's very tenuous…"

Robert Turghoff groaned. "Patty, I know this is not in your job description…but given the delay here, would you be willing to give me a bit of a massage. Just a touch on the back. The problem is right in the middle…"

"You're not listening."

He had turned sideways on the couch and was trying to point in the general direction of the pain.

"I *am* listening. Really, I am. Here, just a couple of minutes. That's all, through the shirt. It's just above where I'm pointing."

Her fingers were tentative at first. But he instructed her, guided her. And finally she began to apply pressure with her thumb, rubbing it along the muscle.

"Oh, yeah. There. There, that's great."

"I think you don't understand," Patty said, her voice coming from behind him. "You have a kind of charisma…"

"What? Charisma? Harder. Really push down on it, you won't hurt me. Are you crazy? Charisma?" His laughter was half groan.

"People want to be around you. I don't know what it is. Maybe they think they can get something from you. Something that will make them more complete."

"Jesus. You've known me what? Almost twenty years now? And you still have no idea. I got about as much charisma as a moldy wash rag. I've been abandoned by everyone I have ever loved. Think about it. My dad run down in a Peoria crosswalk by a drunk when I was twenty-five. To this day no one knows what he was doing there at two in the morning when he was supposed to have been tending bar sixty miles away. I got a silent, demented mother being force-fed in a nursing home. Two wives gone, two kids scattered by the wind. I got a sister I last saw two Christmases ago whose husband suspects I'm a commie. A niece and a nephew who probably couldn't recognize me in a lineup. You call that charisma?"

She was getting into it now. Working the muscles of his lower neck and shoulders. Then the thumbs up and down both sides of his spine.

"Every family has its own dynamic," she said, her voice wistful. "Its own reality, a reality that is almost physical but not quite. A family is a gestalt if you will. You can sense it but you can't actually see it. Maybe it's like those auras we used to talk about, remember?"

"Jen," Turghoff murmured.

Patty giggled. "Of course. I remember asking her at some point how it happened that she should spend a couple of minutes with me in a checkout line and immediately propose that I come live with the two of you and help take care of your precious Marta."

"Your aura."

"Precisely. My aura. But seriously, a family is a real thing. It has an identity that includes the family members but it is more than their separate identities. It is real *as a family*. It has its own motion, its force and strength, its own life span, its own memories, its wounds, its intent, its hopes and dreams."

"Well, mine…," Turghoff said softly, as if to himself. "Mine is hopelessly shattered."

Patty continued without pause as she absently massaged his back: "I imagine a family as a flexible, constantly shape-changing thing that stretches as its members pursue their own goals or flee their own demons, and then it contracts, concentrates, when they rush back to one another.

"And some families, Robert, have more strength. They have more resilience, more flexibility than others. That's what I'm trying to tell you. Yvonne's family is fragile. And you have strength and force. You possess a gravitational pull, whether you appreciate it or not. If you enter the orbit of the Curtiss family you will change it. You will distort it. You may destroy it."

Robert Turghoff felt sad, emptied and alone. Family was apparently Patty's favorite subject. And he had none. Not after the day his Jen drove to Eureka to get a pap smear and returned to announce that she had fallen in love with her doctor. It had seemed that sudden and incongruous at the time. One day he had a family and the next day he did not.

But later, after Jen and the kids and the doctor had decamped for Colorado and he had rented out his house to a rich young couple from San Francisco who wanted a weekend getaway, and had fled to Italy where in his junior year of high school he had been an exchange student, he came to realize that the destruction of his family had been more complicated than that. Much more complicated. It was not, as he had first believed, just some evil, manipulating gynecologist whose skillful fingers turned his wife away from him. No, it had to do with the very family thing Patty was going on about. That mysterious phenomenon whose mundane complexities he could never quite understand or appreciate, and he had found easier to take for granted.

Wandering in Italy that spring, as he prowled through museums and darkened chapels to study the old masters, he had come to realize that what destroyed his marriage had been the little things that kept him from his work: the mild irritants like leaving the studio when called to dinner, or setting down his brush to go pick up Vince from school, or listening to Jen complain about hassles at her work, or just sitting on the floor and playing with Marta for an hour. His art had come first. It pulled at him. He had to force himself to get away, and when away he leaned toward getting back. He had been painting when the family bus left the station and he had not looked up or said goodbye or heard the sound or even smelled the exhaust until long after it was gone.

Turghoff released a long slow breath. "I understand there was an accident," he said to Patty.

"Yes, there was an accident."

CHAPTER EIGHT

"I was in an accident," Yvonne said when she turned to face him.

He wanted to get back to the sketch and was not inter-ested in hearing about her aches and pains. Everyone had aches and pains, and most everyone, it seemed, wanted to talk about them.

"I could put a cushion on the stool if that would help," he suggested. She had a natural grace that somewhat awed him. The way she stood there looking chagrined, her bag held absently in her hand, the elbow bent, her legs slightly parted, weight more on the right, her shoulders broad. If he could persuade her to return to the stool, how would she sit? Would she place herself naturally in the same position, or would he have to reposition her? He would do that if he had to, but the assumed pose was never quite the same as the natural one. Shaping the subject created a resistance. She would no longer be a person sitting on a stool. She would have become a model holding a pose.

Turghoff found a seat cushion and placed it on the stool, patting it down with his hand. Yvonne set her bag on the table and obediently returned to where he stood.

"I'm sorry. I'll be all right now."

She sat down and there it was, like magic, the same exact position. He felt a certain suspicion when he recognized what she had done. Either she possessed a completely natural grace or she was a professional model or a person engaged in some obscure calculation that perhaps even she was not fully aware of. He picked up the charcoal and returned to work.

"You want to talk about the accident?" he asked. Anything, he thought, to keep her where she was.

She, her husband and their daughter, who was nine at the time, had gone fishing, she told him, on the Russian River one Sunday at a place not far from Monte Rio. It was spring and the shad were running. Her husband liked to fish. It was in his blood. He had grown up in a fishing family. Three boys, a father who fished. Before she met him she had never done anything like that. No camping, no fishing, no hikes in the woods. She would have been hard pressed to distinguish a reel from a rod. Her parents were the opposite of Gil's.

"My parents play bridge, host elaborate cocktail parties organized around themes; they hire people to plant flowers and mow the lawn." Her dad sold insurance. Her mother had sold real estate for a short while but then quit.

"So she's a housewife, your mother?"

"Hardly a housewife. She manages house cleaners, window washers, lawn maintenance guys. She's a socialite, that's how she would describe herself. Very social, very gregarious. Constantly on the phone. Organizing events. Running off to coffee klatches. She's a nervous wreck if she's caught alone somewhere, cut off from her friends. I am nothing like my mother. Not either one of them. Really! I know I'm not adopted but for years I thought I had to have been. It was a private horror I carried around inside myself. Who are these people? How did I end up in this family?"

So on that Sunday morning, she and her husband had parked their car off the side of the road and were climbing down an embankment to the river carrying all their gear, their beer and food, stuff for Carly. Carly was complaining so Yvonne picked her up and was carrying her when her foot slipped and she lost her balance.

"It happened so quickly. Even now it's just a blur. I'm falling. I'm holding onto Carly so I don't drop her and I'm twisting around to keep from landing on her. The outside part of my left foot hits hard on the edge of a sharp rock. I hear this snapping sound and the next thing I know I'm on my back head down toward the river with Carly on top of me. When Gil comes back he sees a ragged edge of white bone sticking out of my leg. Came right through the skin. Gil says I took one look at that bone and passed out dead away. I don't remember that part."

"Tibia?" Turghoff asked, sketching.

"Both of them."

"Ouch."

"Tell me about it. As a teenager I was anorexic. That was the day I learned that my bones have been fucked. My teeth are too, but I had already known that. But the leg was not the worst part. When I landed, I also chipped two vertebrae at the base of my neck. The EMT gang finally got there. They strapped me on a board and hauled me away to emergency."

She stopped talking, having completed her obviously oft-repeated tale, and Turghoff found himself puzzled. The woman was a walking disaster. Anorexic? What horrors, he wondered, had brought that on? A stranger in her parents' home, her teeth and bones destroyed, operations and months of rehab. And now she could not sit still for ten minutes without having to jump up and pop a pill. And yet, there she sat, seemingly at ease, a picture of grace.

It was not supposed to play out that way. He prided himself on his ability to read bodies, to look at the surface and discern the subtext. She appeared too comfortable in her skin to have that history locked inside. There should be some tightness, some evidence that she had armored herself against fear. Her history demanded a twitch, a jitter in the eye.

And maybe there was. Maybe he had just not found it yet. Turghoff had begun the sketch with an overall contour, a shaping of the composition: a woman sitting somewhat provocatively on a stool. But the legs and feet had so fascinated him that to that moment he had paid little attention to anything above the knees. The remainder no longer interested him that much, frankly. Completing the portrait would just be a task now, he realized, like setting bricks into a wall that had already been designed, measured and marked off.

But Yvonne Curtiss, who at that moment seemed lost in quiet reverie, was expecting a complete portrait. He had offered that. She would want it to possess a perfect likeness, though idealized, no doubt. "Not my feet!"

He felt himself in a quandary. As he learned when he put in the swimming pool, once a wall is designed and lined out and the ground leveled, you can build the actual wall in a state of absent contentment, radio blaring, casual conversation, slapping on the mortar, pressing the bricks down and squaring them in place. But a portrait could not be done absently. At times you could fill in the background of a painting that way. You might polish a stone carving that way if you were cautious. He had observed skilled furniture makers—men and women who worked with a degree of precision that was completely foreign to him—whistle and joke as they worked. But you cannot do a portrait of a woman that way. At least he could not.

So he said to her: "Do you swim? I have a pool out back."

"Are you?"

"Finished? Not at all, but I need a break."

"I don't have…"

"It's walled in," he explained. "I built it myself. It's completely private out there."

59

At the deep end of the pool Turghoff peeled off his T-shirt and dropped his shorts and dove in. He did this daily when the weather allowed. He could easily swim the length underwater, and did, and when he had reached the far end and surfaced and turned, she was already in the water, doing a clumsy dogpaddle toward safer, shallower territory.

CHAPTER NINE

The girl was twelve when Yvonne brought her to the studio. Turghoff offered his hand, and Carly, uneasy with such formality, extended her own, keeping her eyes down. She was a thin child. The word "spindly" entered his mind, not critically, but in the sense of new growth, the filling out would come later. She was in the early spring of her life and puberty approached with its rush of confusing energy.

He noticed her long lashes immediately. Her hair was dark like her mother's, long and slightly wavy, and was held in place by two plastic turquoise-colored barrettes. The color of the barrettes matched the bracelet on her left wrist and the coloring of her shorts and sandals. Her mother had described her as "artistic." She had prepared herself for this outing, he realized.

But she was shy, and to escape the tension went quickly to Jocko, his old cat, who was curled up on one of the stuffed, throw-away chairs he kept out there for kibitzers and drinking buddies. Her movement toward the cat reminded him of Jocko himself, who when he became nervous would look away and begin to scratch himself as if he had not a care in the world. She approached the sleeping cat patiently, crouching on the gritty floor and reaching out to lightly stroke between Jocko's ears.

"Carly loves animals," Yvonne said.

The girl seemed almost reluctant when they led her to the portrait he had placed on an easel beneath one of the skylights.

"When I let your mother see this for the first time…"

"He wouldn't let me see it forever…" Yvonne broke in.

"Let me tell this," he insisted.

"Yes."

"When I let your mother see this for the first time, and, yes, it is true, I would not let her see it until I was finished, or nearly so."

"Three sittings!" Yvonne blurted out.

"Yes. But what I'm trying to say…" Turghoff touched his fingers to his chest. "The drawing is my work, you see. It is my creation. Had I let your mom, or any model, start commenting on the drawing while I was doing it, then it would no longer be my work. Does that make sense?"

The girl shook her head, glancing at her mother.

"Well, your mom's comments, her suggestions, would have affected me and that would have had an effect on the drawing." The girl's dazed look caused him to persist, "Her comments would have changed the way I saw the drawing and that would have changed the way I finished it. As a result the drawing would not have been completely mine anymore. It would have become 'our' drawing, in some way, both your mom's and mine."

The girl and her mother stared at the portrait with baffled expressions. Turghoff felt a wave of frustration pass through him. How incompetent he believed himself to be with words.

"Okay," he said, starting again, "I am confusing you, but this is important and I will try to explain it better. First, when your mom says this is "her" portrait, that is not correct. I own the drawing. I may give it to her. I may not. But for now, it is mine. Does that part make sense?"

"Of course, it's your drawing," Yvonne said, embarrassed and annoyed, as if he were exposing some greed in her. Turghoff brushed his hand across her shoulder in what he hoped appeared an innocent gesture and was relieved to see Carly nod her head.

"Good. The second thing is, your mother may call this "her" portrait meaning that the drawing is a portrait I made of her, but that is not completely true either. It is not just that I own the drawing, I mean something else. The model I used to make the drawing is not the same as the subject of the drawing. The subject of the drawing is some combination of the model and what is in my head at the time I make the drawing. The subject is a combination of the model and the artist, but more as well, more than your mother and more than me."

No sign came that either of them comprehended any part of this. Yvonne shifted her weight from one foot to the other. Carly glanced around as if anticipating a run for Jocko.

Turghoff felt something like despair at that moment. The three of them stared haplessly at the drawing as if it were some inexplicable object they had come upon by accident.

"So, I looked at the model, in this case your mother, and I perceived an image. But that image got filtered through me, the artist. It passed through my head, through my imagination, and finally through my fingers, and in the process the image changed. It picked up impressions, parts of me as I was at that moment, and what came out, what ended up on the paper, was not just your mother's image and not just me. The image on the paper is a new thing in the world; it's a drawing, a work of art. We may judge it to be a good drawing, or a bad one, but it is a new creation. It is not just your mother as she looked that after-noon sitting on the stool, that's my point. Do you understand?"

The girl shook her head.

"Robert…" Yvonne started to speak and again Turghoff cut her off. He felt himself a fool but he had to go on.

"No, this is important. Carly can understand this."

"How is she supposed to understand it?" Yvonne said. "I can't."

"Okay, think of it this way. I could never have done this drawing if I had not met your mother. That's obvious, right?"

"Uh huh."

"Good. So, does the drawing look like her?"

Carly looked up at her mother as if making a comparison but really, it was obvious, to get permission.

"Sort of."

"Exactly! Sort of! Yes, exactly." Turghoff felt transformed. "Your mother was the inspiration for the drawing. She was the model I used to create the drawing. She sat on that stool over there and I stood over here and I made this drawing. But I am not a camera. I am not a copy machine. I was not trying to perfectly reproduce your mother on the paper. I'm an artist!"

Carly and Yvonne looked at each other, baffled, perhaps alarmed in some way.

Turghoff took a deep breath; he shook his head causing his hair to fly about.

"So, Carly, tell me. How does the drawing *not* look like your mother?"

The girl glanced at her mother again and then at the floor. They were both staring at the floor, he realized. The grave he was digging for himself kept getting deeper and deeper.

"Do you know the silver chain your mother wears around her neck sometimes? The one that has a little key on it?"

Carly looked up and nodded.

"Do you see it in the drawing?"

She studied the drawing for a long time; then she looked at her mother and said, "Maybe."

"I like your answer," Turghoff said. "Where do you see the key?"

The girl pointed.

"Very good. So, is the key larger or smaller than your mother's key?"

"Bigger."

Turghoff nodded happily. The key had come out much larger than the one Yvonne had been wearing that afternoon. The key he had drawn resembled one that might be used to open or close an ancient door, a prison, a church. And the chain was heavier. What on Yvonne had been a delicate ornament had in his drawing become a symbol of authority.

The portrait, he now realized, had power but it was a mess. It failed because it was not really one work of art, but two. It was a creation started by one artist—the one who had drawn those innocent damaged feet with their casual, graceful balance—but completed by another. The second artist had created a slightly older, slightly heavier woman, beautiful in her way, but powerful, an abbess, a mother superior. The first artist had completed his work before their swim; the second had done his after. The second artist, he saw now, had been frightened. He had felt himself under the influence of a powerful emotion, one that both attracted and terrified him.

"Is there anything else you notice that's different?" Robert Turghoff now bravely asked the young Carly Curtiss.

"The nose is different," she said with some confidence.

She was right about that as well. The nose he had not gotten quite right.

CHAPTER TEN

Robert Turghoff lay face down on Solomon's chiropractic table, chin to cushion. He could smell the cleanser that Solomon had sprayed on the table after the last patient left. The sanitary aroma was oddly comforting as he awaited the feel of Solomon's hands. The spasms were gone, thanks to Patty. He did not really need an adjustment, it seemed to him. He needed a healing. And Solomon was a healer. That which Solomon touched got better.

What seemed obvious to Turghoff—and he had told this to Solomon on several occasions—was that Solomon was a healer, not really a chiropractor. After a couple years of driving nails into wood and giving his customers the neck and shoulder massages they were always asking for, he had gone off to Iowa for four years to get a degree that meant nothing in the real world except a license to stick on a wall and the right to charge fees for what he used to do for free, namely heal people with his hands. Solomon would never admit to this, just as he did not admit that Patty ran the operation, but both were true.

As usual Solomon wanted to talk about wine. Specifically, pinot noir, and more specifically a ton of pinot grapes they could buy from a guy Solomon knew in the Anderson Valley. He wanted Turghoff to go halves with him. Pinot and chardonnay were the first to ripen and the man was telling Solomon the pinot should be ready by the end of August. When he called to say the grapes were ripe they would have to jump into Turghoff's truck and drive down to the vineyard. They would bring the grapes back to Solomon's place where he would supervise the process. But Turghoff would end up with half the wine.

"How well do you know this guy?"

"Three years. And I know the vineyard. I've walked through it. Good ground. I was there for the harvest last year. I tasted the grapes. That's when I put in my bid. He says the crop is looking good. The skins are becoming a little slack, the seeds are starting to turn, the BRIX is climbing steadily; should come to twenty-four or even better. It will cost us a grand each for the grapes."

Turghoff did not know. He was not feeling plush but he liked the idea of it.

"Will he take cash for my half?" he asked, thinking of the buried quart jars.

"If he won't I will," Solomon said. He stepped to Turghoff's side and placed his soft hands across the back of Turghoff's neck.

That was a strange thing about Solomon's hands. They had a gray fleshy appearance and his right when you shook it felt soft, almost like the hand of a politician. But great strength was hidden in there. Healing hands.

Turghoff felt a pop and then an effervescent sense of release, and with the release came images of Yvonne Curtiss that flashed like lightning strikes through his consciousness. Following the images, trailing along like eager puppies, were emotional sensations. It was causal, he realized. The pressure caused the pop and the sensations were what the pressure had released. The sensations threw light on the problem that had created the tension in the first place.

No, that was not fair, he said to himself. Problem was not the right word. Yvonne was not a problem, nor was she the cause of the tension. It was like the drawing he had so unsuccessfully tried to explain to Carly. Yvonne was not the cause of the tension any more than she was the subject of the drawing. Yvonne was just Yvonne, this stranger who had come to his studio one afternoon to interview him for the local paper. He, not she, had produced the tension, just as he had produced the drawing that ended up on the paper.

All of this occurred to him while Solomon placed his hands here and there on Turghoff's back.

"Your wife and boss and our dear Patty, seems to believe that I have become an interloper. That I am about to destroy a marriage. You probably know nothing about this but I want you to know that destroying a marriage is not my intent. Patty is not correct about this. I am not in fact some scorpion-like creature who shoots toxic juices into anyone who gets near me. If the subject comes up the next time you and she are touching fingers in the popcorn bowl, I hope you will defend me on this subject."

Solomon's hands paused, then pressed down hard and Turghoff experienced again that moment in the pool when he had reached out his hand and for the first time touched Yvonne's cheek. They were facing each other, standing in water to their shoulders both breathing heavily from the swim. A strand of dark wet hair had fallen across her left eye and he had reached out and folded it back behind her ear. Then he had brushed his hand along her cheek, and in that moment something inside him had shuddered and moved as if awakening from a long sleep.

"The Curtiss family. Carly's mom and dad," Solomon said.

"That's the one."

Solomon's hands paused now at the base of his spine, resting on the small vertebrae that trailed off like the remnants of a tail. Turghoff felt a certain apprehension. There was something dangerous about this. At times, Solomon's healing took place along a risky edge of injury. While his hands were soft, his shoulders were thick and strong and he understood leverage, and he could exert great and sudden force where needed, or where he felt was needed.

Turghoff had had problems before at the base of his spine. Sciatica had erupted after his being crammed into coach during a long flight back from Naples and pain had shot down his right leg when he hobbled off the plane. The focal point had been the exact spot Solomon was now touching. And the treatment he did receive had only made it worse. Sometimes, only time could heal an injury.

"If it were me, I'd run," Solomon said. "I'd run, and I would not look back until I was over the hill and around the corner." Then he pressed and pressed hard.

CHAPTER ELEVEN

Over the next few weeks, Robert Turghoff and Yvonne Curtiss initiated a campaign to transform Turghoff's concept into a completed mural.

In the foreground of the sketch he prepared for the first mural were two large male figures, one a Native, the other a European settler. The sides of the image were dark green, forested with conifers. In the foreground the two figures stood well-lit on opposite sides of an opening; between them the eye followed a path through the forest to a sunlit hill covered with scattered broadleaf trees and golden summer grasses rippling wave-like in the wind. This hillside with its unique outline against the blue sky was drawn to represent the actual hillside against which Long Branch was located. Commonly known as Big Hill, it would, he hoped, be recognized immediately by locals even though Big Hill was today protected and forested with tall conifers, and the ground leading to the hill was no longer a path, but had been divided into streets dotted with houses and utility poles.

Turghoff wanted the two large figures to stand in a relationship to one another that suggested a complexity of moods and possibilities. They should convey dignity, gravity and wariness, but, from the perspective of the viewer, they would be bidding a welcome to the community. This mural could not be sugary, he kept saying, a term he used frequently to express disdain. The past would not be romanticized, not in his mural.

He had toyed with the idea of making one of the figures female and the other male but the concept did not work. His and the community's residual, almost genetic memories of kidnap and rape were too powerful. Either way he tried it, native female with male settler or female settler with a male native, the image evoked in himself and, he assumed, in most viewers, a sense of alarm. The power of it shocked him and while Turghoff admired artistic creations where the unspoken rose to stun the viewer, it would not work for a public mural such as this.

Yvonne suggested the idea of two children, one male and one female who have just happened upon each other. The native girl is carrying a beautiful woven basket while the settler boy has some tool in his hand. Not a gun, a bucket perhaps or a small hatchet. But Turghoff rejected the idea out of hand. "If they are pubescent then we are back to rape and pillage," he said.

"No, ten, eleven-year-olds," she countered. "You could portray them with just a hint of romance. I know you could." She was teasing him.

"Rape and pillage," he insisted. "And if they are younger, then the whole thing will turn sugary to the point of nausea. Norman Rockwell on steroids. The tourists who see this mural will have pulled into town to grab a bite of food. We don't want them throwing up in the gutter before they get to the café."

"Then what about two adult females," Yvonne argued. "A woven basket again for the native woman in traditional dress. Perhaps a wooden pail for the settler, she with her bonnet, her full skirt and heavy blouse. Talk about dignity."

The idea had some appeal, he had to admit. But sugary. It would end up being sugary. He preferred two males.

"These men will be armed, suggesting a fluid, volatile situation. Remember the history. There were massacres on both sides, cattle killed, women raped, children stolen away from their families and hauled off to be Christianized and stripped of their heritage. The past is not pretty. It's not charming or cute. And we are the product of that past, you and I. All of us. America was built out of that ugliness, formed from that rotting, putrid clay. It is in our genes. It's the source of our strength, our insane ambition, our endless lust for violence. I want there to be tension in this mural. I want gravity. I see two powerful male figures with radically different histories confronting one another not in violence, but with a wary, dignified restraint. Yes, that is what I want."

"So, we women are shunted aside again." Yvonne was no longer teasing. He could tell she felt it personally and it angered her.

"The second mural, the next one will be that mural, the one you suggest. The two women. I like the idea of the two women the way you describe them. The outfits, the basket, the pail. I like all of it. Perhaps I could position them beside the river, each coming for water, each surprised by the other. Something in their positions, their expressions, might suggest the first hint of accommodation. But not in this first one. I want the tension, the sense of underlying but restrained violence."

She was not buying it. "You talk about history, Turghoff, but that's y*our* history. You are perpetuating your *male* history. Don't you see that? You are just like every other man. You are putting us off, shunting us aside. Telling us to wait until some other time, until the time is right. Second place has to do for us women. It's second place, or it's no place at all."

Yvonne reached into her purse and pulled out the now-familiar white bottle, removed a pill and swallowed it.

"And was there some sort of accommodation?" she asked, with what seemed to him a cynical tone. "You haven't spoken of accommodation before."

"No," he admitted. "There was no accommodation. Some European men took up with Native women but who knows what that was like, or what lay behind it."

"We can guess," she said sourly. "And as you well know, there may never be a second mural."

Turghoff acknowledged her point with a slight nod. He had been through two marriages and enough other affairs of the heart to not respond. He would not demean himself by blurting out some nonsense about how there would be a second mural, how he would see to that. To do so would have been flatulent and false, he thought, humiliating both to himself and to her. Let it go, let it go.

But while his mouth closed, his mind continued to race. This was his mural, damn it. He appreciated her help, but the project was his. The artwork was his, the concept was his and he had a right, even an obligation to protect it. He felt an existential duty in that regard. He was not simply defending his project, he was defending who he was, as an artist, as a man. Besides, it was not his job to change the course of human history, to right its endless wrongs. His job was to bring this concept, his concept, into reality.

It was late afternoon and she would be leaving soon, back to her husband and daughter. They stood at the counter in the kitchen of his house, each holding a glass of wine. Seen through the windows of the breakfast nook, the angled sun struck the apple tree with stunning force. But inside, being on the eastside of the house, the kitchen's interior light had faded and the coloring had taken on a softness that pleased him.

They were in the midst of a torrid affair that had begun in the pool and had not faded. Her capacity for passion in the act of lovemaking humbled him. She seemed capable of entering a different realm from the one they occupied day to day—and taking him with her.

She looked away now. Angry? Hurt? Disappointed? Perhaps she had imagined that he would be different from other men and he was proving her wrong. But really, he had no idea what she was thinking. Maybe she was blaming herself for pushing so hard. He only knew what he felt, and looking at her now, seeing on her face an expression that mystified him, he felt himself filling with desire. Even an argument, it seemed, served as an aphrodisiac. Especially an argument.

She drank off her remaining wine and set the glass on the counter. "I have to go," she said, as if she had read his mind.

CHAPTER TWELVE

During the six months he spent in Italy following the breakup of his family, Robert Turghoff had tried to discover the seed hidden at the center of the painter Caravaggio. The artist, dead now four hundred years, perplexed and fascinated him. Here was a man who, it seemed to Turghoff, possessed no real passion for being an artist but was still a genius with great technical skill and a powerful sense of dramatic story. He used these gifts to make money and to worm his way into the higher reaches of society, but his real passions lay elsewhere.

Turghoff, by contrast, had always wanted to be a painter; it was what he lived for. He knew he was an artist before he knew how to draw, a painter before he knew how to paint. But what Caravaggio wanted to be, and what he proved himself to be, was a tough guy with a sword or dagger. Based on what Turghoff had learned, that was his heart's calling. Probably gay, most certainly tormented, Caravaggio sheltered in the homes of noble patrons but roamed rough streets ready to brawl.

He fled Rome after killing a man with a dagger, and, after a stop in Naples, made his way to Malta hoping to be accepted into the Knights of St. John. The Knights were seriously tough guys, defenders of the faith, warriors against Islam, and he wanted to be one of them. But his predilection for violence accompanied him to Malta, and again he had to flee. Shortly after returning to Naples Caravaggio departed by boat for Rome. With him was a painting he had made for the pope. With this gift he hoped to be forgiven for the murder and allowed back in Rome. But death had other ideas, and Caravaggio never made it to Rome.

Toward the end of his brief tormented life, the man painted dark, tension-filled, flesh-exposed masterpieces. Turghoff found many of these creations painfully grotesque, and yet so compelling as to be almost frightening. To look upon a Caravaggio it was—or so it seemed at the time—as if he were seeing forbidden images from which he could not divert his eyes. How could such allure arise from such ugliness, and how had Caravaggio accomplished this work though his identity, his desires, lay elsewhere? Turghoff, at that time himself tormented and riven with loss, had been fascinated.

And now years later, back in sunny California and contemplating his first mural, Turghoff remembered *The Seven Acts of Mercy*, one of Caravaggio's most famous altarpieces. Located in Naples in a dark and rather dingy building, the painting when he saw it was situated behind an altar ten or more yards from where a viewer could stand. The painting was a disaster, it seemed to him. Its dusty surface, over-crowded with characters and events, was extremely dark both physically and emotionally. To understand it at all one needed an explanation and a diagram, or lacking a diagram, a coin to activate a little machine that projected onto a screen the various scenes in the actual painting.

It only made sense to Turghoff to see *The Seven Acts of Mercy* as a depiction of hell on earth, but the depiction housed a contradiction. Filled with shadowy figures in distress, the painting portrayed one woman and several men performing the seven acts of mercy: burying the dead, visiting the imprisoned, feeding the hungry, clothing the naked, sheltering the homeless, visiting the sick and giving drink to the thirsty. Caravaggio provided all this plus an angel with magnificent wings hovering above. But it was all darkness. Darkness broken by lightning-like flashes of white and red, folds of cloth, an arm bare, a back twisted, a leg, a breast exposed, the wrinkled soles of a corpse.

Now that he was a mural-man, Turghoff wanted to create a mural that was the opposite of Caravaggio's altarpiece. He wanted to convey a welcome filled with light, clarity and dignity but he also wanted his mural to possess some of the drama the master had so excelled at.

"But no angels," he said to Yvonne after he had shown her a photo of *The Seven Acts of Mercy*. "Not a single angel."

"May I quote you on this?" she asked

§

The next day Robert Turghoff and Yvonne Curtiss drove through Long Branch in his heavy old pickup searching for walls. There were a lot of walls, but walls were not canvases that could be transported to an ideal location. A beautiful wall was useless to support a mural if the only people who saw it were garbage collectors once a week, or if there was no space before it where a viewer could get some perspective. And walls had other problems. The ones that appealed to him tended to be broken up with windows, doors, elaborate entrances. They supported garish signs or were marred by overhangs, gas meters and electrical connections. And the surfaces varied from corrugated metal, to brick, from rotting asbestos to wood while their conditions ranged from nearly new to near collapse.

You could frame a canvas to the shape you wanted, but like its location, the dimensions of a wall were set. They may be tall and thin or short and squat, but Turghoff needed size. The wall for this first mural should be taller than wide but it had to command a view. The two figures needed to catch and hold the eye. Ideally it should be visible to persons taking one of the two off- ramps or it could be positioned downtown itself. Unfortunately, like many American communities, Long Branch had no piazza, no central square, just a main intersection, the only one with stoplights. Main, the east-west street running through the intersection, had most of the older buildings. They were two or three stories high. A couple had false-fronts, several shared walls.

Turghoff felt cramped driving around, frustrated. He jutted his head out the window and then pulled it back; he bent low over the steering wheel. He wanted to find what did not exist: a six-story brick building with no windows fully viewed from the main intersection, or at the outskirts near one of the off-ramps.

All this he lamented to Yvonne, aware that he was venting a fantasy. He knew the town. He had lived there for a quarter century. He remembered when trenches were dug and the power lines buried along Main. He had celebrated when trees were planted, the ones that now shaded the sidewalks and hid the fronts of some of the buildings. And he remembered two major fires. A decrepit nineteenth century hotel built entirely with old-growth redwood had burned to the ground one night the summer he and Alicia arrived. That fire, coming in the dry season, had threatened to reduce the whole place to ash. Then five years later a second fire, this one in the middle of winter, a restaurant located across the street and a block east from where the hotel had been.

He had mourned the loss of that second building, he explained to Yvonne. "I have an old postcard of it somewhere I can show you. A log house with an overhanging shake roof and two large round windows facing the street that had been framed with cross-sections cut from a huge redwood. And the breakfasts! I can still smell the coffee; hash browns, sausage cooking on the grill, grease on everything, loggers lined up on the counter stools, suspenders crossing the striped shirts on their thick backs. Someday, I'll put that image on a mural. The old timers would get a kick out of it."

They got out of the truck and walked Main Street. It was midafternoon and would have been stifling had a wind not come up off the river. But the wind raised dust and Yvonne pulled her dark glasses down from her forehead to protect her eyes.

He showed her the vacant lots where the hotel and restaurant once stood. Debris was scattered about both, the vegetation scruffy and wild. A flimsy lean-to draped with a blue tarp showed bright in the sun at a back corner of the old hotel lot. One or more humans must be living there, he said, pointing it out. Discarded packaging lay around: plastic, paper, cardboard, eye-catching designs fading in the weeds.

From the moment he started to imagine the murals, Turghoff had begun to see the town differently.

"You can feel how the energy has seeped out of down-town and coalesced at the off- ramps where the gas stations, the chain motels and restaurants have sprung up. Travelers stop; they sleep and eat. They fuel their cars. Those are boring places out there, completely sterile! Buildings designed in corporate boardrooms and reproduced from coast to coast without char-acter. They are more brands than buildings, those structures, and no identification with place. For most of the travelers who stop, this town, our town, exists only as an exit number on a road map."

She nodded as they walked down the street and he rambled on. She was careful not to touch him, or walk too close in this public place. She seemed particularly serene to him on this warm afternoon, her tranquility a strong contrast to his own jangled mood. God, he thought, his fit of nostalgia was disgusting; his voice whiny and pathetic. And his complaints about the corporatization of the culture were so trite, so fait accompli.

"It's all bullshit," he said. "I'm sorry."

"No, this is good." She had taken out her notebook and was jotting something down.

Great, he thought, now his every rambling moan threatened to end up on the front page of *The Woeful*.

"Let's take a run up Big Hill," he said, making a sudden turn back toward the truck.

They drove to the top of the hill that he had envisioned as the backdrop of the first mural. The hill was forested and laced with hiking trails but on the far side a road switched back and back again as it climbed to the top. At the summit he pulled onto the graveled overlook and the two of them walked to the edge. They were above and south of the town. They could see Main Street running east and west in front of them. Farther back, the river formed an arcing border at the edge of the community, and beyond the river, mimicking its course, was the freeway. A distant line of hills formed the horizon showing faintly purple with haze.

The freeway had to be two or three miles away but they could hear the traffic. Two semis, he counted, three motorcycles, several passenger cars flying by. Except for the bridges at either end, each with its cluster of services, the river formed a sort of moat that kept the traffic away from the town itself.

At that moment, Turghoff felt himself doubting the very idea of public murals. What was the point? From this perspective the passing traffic had a frantic, feverish energy that he would prefer be kept at a distance. Did they really want to draw those roaring machines into their quiet little community? Even assuming the murals brought some economic gain, would the town become a better or a worse place in which to live? He and most everyone else complained about the empty storefronts, the vacant, weed-filled lots and the motley collection of dead-eyed druggies that had sprouted up and were now part of the town's character. But would anyone really be better off if his project succeeded and the town became a roosting place for tour buses belching fumes and crowds of pastel-colored, loud-voiced seniors with their pointing cameras and desperate need of a toilet?

About this, he was careful to say nothing to the diligent reporter standing beside him. His predicament was truly bizarre. One minute he wanted to stroke her cheek and then next he was afraid to open his mouth.

"I suppose the high school gymnasium is a possibility," she said, breaking his reverie.

CHAPTER THIRTEEN

The gym was a terrible idea and he told her so. Yes, the building was tall and in good condition. And yes, the wall space was unbroken on one side. No doors and the only windows were up near the roof. But the location was not good. Only locals would see it. Besides, he told her, schools were magnets for rage. Look at the school shootings. Put something beautiful there, something the adults make a big deal over, set it right in the students' faces every day and the temptation to vandalize it would be irresistible.

"I thought you wanted to involve the kids. If it's theirs or they are part of it, why would they vandalize it?"

"Because the ones who work on it will not be the ones who vandalize it. Besides, the location is not good. Maybe a later one. But not the first. The first has to be where the traffic is. Besides, I have an idea."

They jumped back into the truck and returned to downtown. As he drove them slowly down Main, he put his arm out the window and pointed. "There!"

He was directing her attention to their left, to the south side of the street. To the east wall of one of the older buildings, one with a false front. The building just east of it was set back a hundred feet with a small parking area in front so the wall he was pointing toward was visible from the street. The building was not tall, two stories and sided with corrugated metal painted an off-white and needing a new coat. At the front lower corner was a window bordered with small lights and displaying toys. But the surface above and to the left of the window was unencumbered wall, two stories of it.

Yvonne did not hide her disappointment. "The toy store? I was imagining something more grand."

So was he. So much for six stories of commanding mural. But this wall was well exposed and only a block from the main intersection.

"And, in that building," he said, pointing again, "the one that's set back…"

"The Tourist and Information office!" she shouted, suddenly getting it.

"Exactly. And the mural will mark the spot."

He pulled the truck into the small parking lot and backed into an empty space so they could view the wall through the windshield. When Yvonne started to speak, he hushed her. He wanted to just be there for a moment. He needed to experience himself inhabiting the space, the parking lot, the wall, the whole place. He wanted to absorb the sense of it.

Yvonne got out of the truck and walked over to the wall. He watched as she ran her hand along the surface. Yes, he understood what she was thinking, the corrugated surface would present a challenge. Then she turned around and was facing him. She struck a dancer's pose, her back to the wall, grinning at him in a manner that was unmistakably flirtatious.

Turghoff had just placed two fingers in his mouth and was about to produce a wolf whistle, a skill he had possessed since childhood, and of which he was absurdly proud, when he heard an adult male voice shout something. He watched as Yvonne dropped her pose and looked with sudden alarm toward the street. There, stopped in the middle of Main Street, was a large blue NewFuel propane truck. And in the driver's seat sat a large man wearing a shirt, the color of which matched the truck. The driver, Turghoff realized, had to be Yvonne's husband.

The man had a puzzled expression on his face. What was his wife doing all alone in full view of everyone on Main Street, dancing around seductively in front of a wall? Obviously, the husband had not seen Turghoff who fortunately had not whistled and continued to sit quietly in his own truck. As he watched somewhat fascinated, Turghoff recognized that the composition, of which he was a part, contained all the ingredients required for a country ballad: two men, two trucks, one woman. He liked the feeling it gave him. There she was dancing around for him, and there sat her husband watching, confused, uncertain. It made him tingle; it gave him a rush.

Yvonne turned toward the street. She held her hands out with an expression of annoyance as if to say: And what are you doing? Aren't you supposed to be working? What Turghoff heard her yell was: "Later!"

As a man who had endured and helped create the failure of two marriages, he could imagine how "later" might transpire. Back at the house that evening, Yvonne would not mention the episode, but if her husband did, she would immediately take the offensive.

"And what were you doing, yelling at me like that? Stopping that huge truck in the middle of Main Street, yelling your head off? And I've got this important man I'm interviewing for his project and all of a sudden there's this guy in a big truck yelling at me? What's he supposed to think about that?"

"I thought you were alone and I couldn't understand what you were up to," the husband would say, still confused, maybe a little suspicious, but somewhat chastened.

"No, I was not alone! He was right there. He saw the whole thing."

"Oh." Shamed, but inside sensing something more. Not wanting to sense it. Annoyed with himself for sensing it. Thinking it a sign of his failure as a human being to be sensing it, but sensing it just the same.

Or maybe it would transpire differently, Turghoff thought. Maybe the husband would go so far as to lie to her and to himself: "I just saw you there and I was happy to see you and so I yelled a greeting, that's all."

And she would smile and reach out and touch his face, and both would be conflicted: guilty and angry and living a sham, but sympathetic, each drawn toward the other for a moment. But the moment would feel tenuous. The image that came to Turghoff was of a couple skating together on an ice-covered lake. The ice was thin. They could feel it flex slightly as they moved farther from shore; they could hear the sounds as it began to crack. Beneath the ice was great pain. They knew the pain was there; they had fallen into it before. They could not keep that icy water out of their minds.

Yes, he had skated on that lake. He knew how it felt for Yvonne and her husband out there on the ice.

§

It would be later that night when Turghoff fabricated the confrontation between Yvonne and her husband in their home, a home he had never seen and did not care to see. He would be in bed, alone in an empty house, and what he felt toward Yvonne and her husband was compassion. What he did not feel was personal responsibility. Or guilt.

The disconnect between his feelings and the imagined domestic scene was similar to the disconnection when he studied one of Caravaggio's great paintings: *The Martyrdom of Saint Matthew*, say, or *The Conversion of Saint Paul.* He would be in awe of the emotions the genius could produce in him on a flat surface covered with paint that had been applied hundreds of years before. Strokes of paint that portrayed a scene from a religion he felt no allegiance to. The emotions were both real and potent, but they were not personal, not in the sense that he had a relationship with the artist or the action portrayed in the paintings.

Earlier he had felt other things. After her husband drove off in the NewFuel rig, Yvonne had come back to the pickup. She got in, banged closed the noisy door, and as he was turning the key, she had placed her hand on his thigh, pushing her fingers up beneath his baggy shorts. He had driven straight to his house. Not a word had been spoken, or needed to be.

Later, the two of them poolside, naked and wet from a swim, she had pulled the white plastic bottle from her purse. She removed a small pink pill and swallowed it. Then she offered him one.

"I'm all right," he said, absently.

"You just think you are. Take one of these and you'll know just how far from 'all right' you are."

The expression on her face in the afternoon light was teasing but hesitant, and, it seemed to him, somewhat sinister. He realized how staid and cautious he had become. Back in his early twenties he would have popped that pill into his mouth without a question asked or a moment's hesitation. I will take the invitation, his actions would have proclaimed. I will be open to the moment. I know you must let go of one swinging trapeze if you hope to grab another—and if you do—and if you do—for an instant there, you will be flying freely through empty air. And in this world, there was no sensation quite like that.

Yvonne had taken a risk by inviting him to join her. She wanted him to come along. It was a plea, really. Come, enter my interior world. It is a world more private, more intimate, more personal than even the lively sex we have just enjoyed.

Turghoff cared about her. Maybe he was coming to love her. But he was not prepared to go where she wanted him to go. Her offer was a lie and he knew it even if she did not. The pill would not deliver him into her internal world. It would take him into his. They would be more isolated, not less. Her promise was an illusion.

He did not ask what the pill was. It did not matter. He just begged off and his refusal wounded her. She had made herself vulnerable and maybe she felt betrayed. He noticed a wince cross her eyes as if he had inserted a needle under her skin. And he experienced that hopeless sensation you get when you realize that something you have done has caused the person you care about to distance themselves from you. From you and the decision you made, and there was nothing you could do now to reduce the distance.

To cover her disappointment Yvonne Curtiss leaped to her feet and dove into the water. She was an awkward diver and a lousy swimmer. But she possessed a bravado that he admired.

CHAPTER FOURTEEN

A few days later she came by with Carly. He had found out who owned the building on whose wall he wanted to paint the mural. The building was one of the oldest in town, he told her, perhaps the oldest. It had served as a harness shop, a post office, a general store. The present tenants, a couple in their fifties, sold a variety of toys and sports equipment out the front and stored their inventory in the rear.

The original structure, which now comprised the front of the building, had been moved more than a hundred years earlier from a location at the river's edge, and the town had developed around it. With winter floods and summer stagnation, the river had proven less navigable and more dangerous than the initial settlers thought and the community had relocated itself to higher ground.

"The owner is a trust or something in San Francisco," he told Yvonne. "Nobody connected with the building lives here anymore, though an ancestor, long dead now, had the building constructed and served as postmaster. That's what the toy people told me. It's managed by an attorney in the City. They send their checks to the attorney, and that is who they call if something needs to be fixed."

"Have you called him?"

"It's a woman."

"Where's Jocko?" Carly wanted to know.

Turghoff turned his attention to the girl. "Jocko? Good question. But I know how to find him. Come with me." He led her into the kitchen where he found a can of tuna and a spoon and offered them to her. She held a large manila envelope in her hand which she set on the table when she took possession of the tuna and spoon.

"A woman?" Yvonne asked, following them into the kitchen.

"The attorney. Beat these together, that's Jocko's dinner bell. And what's in here?" He pointed toward the envelope.

"Just some…"

"She brought some drawings to show you."

"Your drawings?"

Carly nodded, embarrassed. Then she began to hit the can with the spoon.

"Louder. Give it a few good whacks."

Turghoff sat down at the table and took the envelope in his hands. It worked like a charm, of course. A moment later, Jocko had squeezed his way through the cat door and was hustling toward the kitchen.

"The fat-cat shuffle," he said, frowning. "So, open the can and give him a little. Not all of it. Just a bit. Put the rest in the refrigerator. His dish is over there."

"Well, have you called?"

He lifted his hand to silence her. He was studying the drawings now. There were five in the envelope, all done with colored pencils, and they were magical. He had learned a long time ago that when you look at a work of art, what you see in the image, in addition to the technique, the style and skill, is the mind of the artist. A work of art allows you to witness the artist's mind at play, its patterns, its shapes and movements.

Carly had that girl-child neatness about her. His own daughter, Marta, had been just like that at her age. He watched as she gave Jocko a bit of food and then closed the can and placed it in the refrigerator. She took the spoon to the sink and washed it off. Then she washed and dried her hands, and returning to the cat, squatted down and began to stroke the top of its head.

"Not yet," he said to Yvonne. "I thought I would start with the Tourist and Information people. They can be a great help here. The mural will be good for them and they should be good for the mural. Once I have their endorsement I will call and speak to the lawyer. The toy shop people like the idea. There's a board, I understand, at the T&I office. Business people, mostly. I know some of them. The idea is to meet with them first."

"Are you ready to put the sketch in the paper? Mel Kline says we have room this week."

"How large? Not if it's going to be squeezed into some corner. That would do more harm than good."

"No large, a quarter page."

"Really? Well, sure, why not?"

"I said to him, 'Do we really need another four photos from last week's football practice?'" She was pleased, proud of herself.

Turghoff brushed his hand along her arm and turned toward the child. "Come here, Carly. Sit by me. I want to talk to you about these drawings." He grabbed a chair and pulled it closer to his. "Here, sit here."

"They're old," she said when she sat down. "I did them when I was five and six, mostly. Right, Mom?"

"Yes, about that."

The drawings were of creatures such as had never existed on this planet. Some had long sweeping tails at each end of their bodies. With others their long-nailed feet faced in opposite directions, as if they were capable of walking away from themselves like those coiled metal slinkies he had known as a kid that could walk themselves down a set of stairs. The bodies themselves were large and arced and had spikes dancing along their backs like mountains along a horizon. The heads were small with perky ears and glancing eyes and snake-like tongues protruding out the front. The lines were graceful and sure, and the compositions bold and straightforward, the colors full of light, whimsy and joy.

He looked at them a long time, picking them up one by one and setting them down.

"Do you still draw?" he asked her.

She shook her head. "Not much, not anymore. That was before we moved. I was little." She was looking at her mother now.

"Yes," Yvonne said. "Well before."

"Well, I want you to come here whenever you wish. Come here to the house or back to the studio. I will give you paper and pens, brushes, paints. Whatever you need, you under-stand? And you will be free to work…"

"Work?"

"Sit and draw. Anything you want to draw. Okay?"

Carly looked at her mother and then nodded her head.

"If I'm not here, Jocko will let you in."

CHAPTER FIFTEEN

Jen, Turghoff's second wife, had come into his life shortly after
Alicia fled back to her rich Boston parents, to central heating
and regular manicures. Alicia had been gone less than three
weeks when he saw a notice Jen had posted on the bulletin board
outside Way Natural, the natural food store that had recently
opened in an abandoned church.

New to Town, the notice had read. Looking for a room
to rent. Need access to kitchen and toilet. Will keep both clean.

He had liked the sound of that. The arrangement lasted
three days before she was staying in his room, though she had
remained true to her word about the cleaning. But since Jen's
departure for Colorado with their two children and her new lady
doctor friend, he had lived alone. It had been seven years now
and he had become quite comfortable with the arrangement.
His skills in the kitchen had developed to the extent that he

dared now and then to invite a guest for dinner. Once a month an undocumented woman he met through Montoya devoted a day to laundry and to thoroughly cleaning the place though the studio remained his sole responsibility. On Saturdays between her visits he did enough to keep the house presentable.

So when Yvonne said, "I don't want anything to happen to my marriage," Turghoff felt a jolt of relief.

Before Yvonne, he had never been involved with a married woman. There was something about the idea that repelled him. So, he told himself, he was not enjoying sex with Yvonne because she was married, but in spite of it. Still, he realized, an affair with a married person while complicated did have built-in controls; her marriage played the role a governor plays on an engine. Turghoff's friend, Bill Watson, an amateur rodeo bulldogger he had known back in the nineties, always claimed that the ideal partner in an affair was a married woman whose husband was in prison. But then Bill had left town suddenly a couple of years later without leaving a forwarding address.

"Or to my husband," Yvonne was saying. "I want you to understand that. Our marriage is not perfect. It's far from perfect. My being here is proof of that, I suppose. But Carly is all I have and she loves her father more than anything in the world and he loves her and…."

Her voice trailed off and Turghoff said, "Tell me about him." They were lying in his bed. He felt like a nap, but if she was talking he could stay awake.

"My husband? Well, his name is …"

"…Gil. Patty told me."

She slapped his chest and then pinched his nose. "So, you've been checking up on us, have you? Doing a little investigative work behind my back?"

He let her accusation stand, though it had been Patty and not he who had brought up his involvement with the Curtiss family. "So, tell me about him," he repeated.

"Gil is a very sweet man. He's still a sweet man, but he was an innocent boy when I met him. Now he's a sweet man who has been badly damaged by his government. He's one of those fools who rushed to join up after the Twin Towers. We were engaged when the planes hit. Those images of brave fire-fighters over and over on the TV, that's what got him. I begged him not to go."

"Fools?"

"Yes, absolutely." She pushed herself off him and sat up, crossing her legs like a yogi, but a yogi more angry than peaceful. "Young men made into fools and sent on a fool's errand. Do you have any idea how many veterans of Iraq and Afghanistan kill themselves every day?"

"He was..?"

"Like twenty every day! Twenty!"

"So, he…"

"Yes, an Army grunt who drove a truck during two tours in Iraq. Have you been there?"

"In the military? No."

"They brainwash you. They absolutely brainwash you. They train you to do things you would not otherwise do and your buddies become everything. They become more important to you than your family, your wife, your child. We got married right away, of course, before he left for basic. I was a fool, too, you see. And then pregnant after the first tour, still a fool.

"But they train it into you and I got trained too. You fall into a nightmare and it all seems perfectly normal. I knew his buddies. I knew their wives, the ones who had them. Your buddies become more important to you than the things that are naturally important. More important than even yourself. Much more important than yourself. And then, when your buddies start getting blown to bits…"

It was silent until Turghoff finally asked, "So, has he…?"

Yvonne nodded. She got off the bed with that smooth unconscious grace that marked most every move she made and that never failed to stun him. She walked to the table and picked up her purse.

"In Santa Rosa a few weeks before we left. I found him sitting naked in the bathtub with a pistol." She removed the bottle and swallowed a pill. "Another five minutes…."

Turghoff pulled a pillow behind him and sat back against the brass work. A smart person would start backpedaling right now. Time for a graceful exit from this pill-popping woman, this armed and suicidal husband, this fragile daughter. Patty had warned him. Solomon had told him to run.

But he felt himself sinking into an unpleasant certainty. It was as if in some other sphere he had given his consent. The hand had been dealt and in some unknowable but inexorable order the cards were being laid on the table, one after another.

In the first days of an affair it seems as though you are playing a game together. (He and Jen had literally crashed into each other in the unlighted house in the middle of the night, he headed toward the john and she coming from. They had joked about that collision for years.) Yes, a game, a joke, a carnival contest with a bit of a dare that offered an orgasm for a prize. But very soon, the entanglements begin. Lives send out tentacles. They reach into the lives of others, and those lives reach into yours. You feel them touching you, changing you; you start to care about people you had not thought to care about before. At least that was the way it had been for him. He had never been accomplished at, or much enjoyed, purchased or quickie sex.

So now his life was to include not just Yvonne Curtiss (double n, double s), but also the fragile daughter, and on the horizon, Gil Curtiss, not just a man yelling from the driver's seat of a large blue truck, but one haunted and naked in a bathtub, pistol in hand.

§

She stood at the table, her back to him and he studied her bottom and the two creases formed at the junction of her buttocks and legs. How graceful were the lines formed by those creases. Yes, the lines were sexual but much more than that. They were beautiful just as lines, bold and graceful in their sweep.

"I just remembered something embarrassing," he said. "Come back. Be with me. Let me tell you."

Back on the bed she laughed and slapped his chest. "The great Turghoff embarrassed, I doubt it."

"No, really, a long time ago. Vince was just a little guy. Marta was an infant, or maybe still in the oven, I don't remember. Anyway, for a while back then Jen took piano lessons from Florence Kline, Mel's mother. We had an upright piano in the living room. It sat against the interior wall, where that large abstract hangs now. After she left I gave the piano away to some guy. Anyway, Jen had a friend named Laura who played flute and they would get together now and then to make music. She and her husband had a couple of small kids in the same daycare so we were friends.

"One day this Laura came over to play and Jen was not back yet. Jen was always running late. So I let Laura in and she took out her flute. She put it together and blew a few notes as we chatted back and forth. Then she went and sat in the window seat, knees up near her chest, her flute in her hands, watching out the window for Jen. Laura was a nice-looking gal, slim. She was wearing a pair of tight slacks, tan, I remember, and I found myself staring at her bottom there on the window seat."

"You lecher," Yvonne said, laughing and slapping him again.

"And she caught me, that's the thing. She caught me staring at her body."

"Lecher!"

"Nothing happened," Turghoff said. "We just kept talking but I knew she had seen me because of the self-satisfied smile that crossed her face. She didn't look at me but the smile was so obvious that I knew she had caught me staring at her bottom."

"Of course she was smiling. She had captured you for a moment, captured the husband of her good friend."

"And I felt this rush of deep shame."

"Well, I should hope so!"

Yvonne started laughing. It was rare she laughed fully, but when she did he was always surprised by it. Her laugh was sudden and full throated, an explosion of energy that shocked and delighted him.

Turghoff pushed himself higher against the pillow and when she had finished he said, "No, you're wrong, that's what I was just thinking. I should not have felt shame at all. I didn't touch her. I didn't say anything. I didn't do anything, I just looked. I was admiring her beauty and we should never be ashamed of admiring beauty."

"You were leching her."

"No, listen to me. That is such a cheap word. There's a level of life that flows just below the surface. You might say it is sexual but I prefer the word sensual. That's the level I was tuning into. It is from there that our sense of the aesthetic emerges. Our sense of beauty is born in infancy, I'm sure of it. When our eyes first start to focus we scan the visual field for those huge, warm, moving shapes that hold and nurture us. How beautiful we must find those shapes."

Yvonne chortled. "So, your mother stuck her butt in your face. Is that what you're telling me?"

"You're being crude, Yvonne. No, the blurry face smiling as it bends toward us, the shoulders moving, that's what creates our aesthetic. The huge hands reaching for us, touching and lifting us, the swollen curves and the fullness of the breast. All our lives we are fascinated by the human body. We find faces in clouds and torsos in chunks of driftwood. Our eyes prowl abstract paintings in search of some hint of the human form. Degas must have spent years painting nude women climbing in and out of bathtubs. Lucian Freud was fascinated by what most think of as the misshapen or ugly. Is this hunger all sexual? Or is it aesthetic? Perhaps sexual desire is just a subset of our unending search for beauty. Yes, our search for beauty is unending. It is what we go through life doing."

Yvonne snickered and shook her head, mocking his sincerity.

"No, listen," he continued. "I had a friend at the Institute, a sculptor. This guy worked out all the time and had a beautiful body. Bulging biceps, pecs, deltoids, and of course, the classic sixpack. I loved looking at Sergei's body. It wasn't sexual, my attraction to his body was aesthetic."

Yvonne shook her head again, black hair waving. "You men are so full of shit, you rationalize the obvious. What fascinated you about your friend was the power his muscles promised. The power to take and destroy. You are predators, Turghoff, underneath, that's what men are. Predators, eager to thrust and penetrate, that's your impulse. You're eager to thrust yourselves into what is not yours. Into women, into countries, into the earth itself for minerals buried beneath the surface."

Yvonne reached over and snapped a fingernail against his limp penis.

"Thrust and penetrate, that's what you're about, buddy boy, that and killing."

It was not a hard snap but it stung, angering him.

"And you?" he said after a moment. "What is the woman's role in all this?"

She looked ecstatic suddenly. "We capture like I said. We capture and enclose. We take your hardness and enclose it and squeeze it for our pleasure. And when the hardness is gone—when it's become useless like that thing—we cast it aside."

Turghoff sighed and then forced a smile. "How sentimental you are, my dear: romance, flowers and chocolates."

He reached over and placed his hand on her. His palm pressed against her vagina, his fingers cupped her bottom. How wonderful it felt to him; she was wet, warm, still relaxed from the sex.

She moaned slightly and squirmed. "Romance? That's surface stuff, Turghoff. We're talking depth here. You gush about some underground river of sensuality straight out of Hallmark, but I've gone deeper. I'm reporting from the tectonic level where the great plates shift, where ancient enemies grapple and embrace, where molten urges rise up and surge white-hot toward the surface of our everyday. That's the male's lair, Turghoff, that's the predator's cave."

He leaned toward her, pressing his hand more firmly against her. "Let me lick on you," he pleaded. "Let me give you another orgasm. Who knows what might rise again."

Yvonne grabbed his hand. She jerked it away and managed to lurch to her feet. "You're being pathetic, Turghoff. Now, you are being truly pathetic."

§

She started to dress herself, looking out the window. Watching from the bed Turghoff recognized something harried and sad about her. It was as if a shade had lifted revealing her tawdry home life with its bills and more bills, the laundry piled up, dishes unwashed in the sink, an unstable husband staring absently at the TV, the fragile child hiding alone in her room. And pain. Pain in the body, pain in the soul, pain that did not go away.

Following her gaze out the window, he saw what she saw: his country place. Against the studio walls, amid August's tall, unmown grasses was a stack of cinder blocks, another of rough-milled redwood four-by-fours set on shims to let the air circulate, and in the weeds his trusty and rusty and dubiously-maintained firewood splitter. Not tidy, even a tad messy, but a pleasant place, a place not filled with pain.

The fire marshal would want him to weed-whack those tall, dried grasses. He should do that, and eventually he would. But he held off, indulging himself in their tall and moving grace.

"I think what you are telling me is that we should break this off," he said now half-heartedly to her back.

It was an offer. A decent thing to do, it seemed to him. Give her an out. Release her back to her family.

"I'll understand," he added weakly.

"Damaged goods!" She turned and she spit the words at him.

"No, I…."

"You've had your fun, now push this fucked up woman back to her fucked up family. That's it, isn't it."

"No, I…"

"Be gone, woman. But, hey, thanks for the fuck. Okay, I get it." She nearly toppled pulling on her jeans.

"Yvonne…"

"And those promises you made to Carly? 'Come by anytime!' 'I'll give you paints? I'll give you brushes?' I suppose that's history too?" She was stumbling around trying to push her feet into her sandals.

Turghoff got off the bed. He put his arms around her. After a moment's resistance, she collapsed against him sobbing.

Her tears wet his bare shoulder, her back trembling against his forearms. Thoughts in his head saying: *This can't go on. Sooner or later this is going to blow sky high.*

CHAPTER SIXTEEN

The board governing the Tourist and Information office met in their small lobby, the five of them seated at a table surrounded by racks of brochures and maps. Turghoff sat nervously at one end with several copies of the sketch he had printed on his large-format printer. He hated meetings and had slept restlessly in anticipation of this one.

Part of the problem was the way he had organized his life following the breakup with Jen and after he returned from Italy. He typically went to bed at nine in the evening, got up shortly after midnight and worked in his studio until dawn. Then he enjoyed a second sleep that ended around eleven at which time he downed two cups of coffee along with a plate of bacon, eggs and toast. When he stepped away from the table at midday it was often with a sense of pleasant anticipation. While thoughts of the current painting might percolate through his mind, he did not need to confront it again until the early hours of the next day.

"Ten in the morning?" he had joked to Yvonne. "What a ridiculous time of day to hold a meeting."

The board members were chatting aimlessly as he twitched and fiddled with his sketches and the scheduled start-time came and went. He heard about vacations taken and planned, about children and grandchildren visiting and traveling, about a sale on shoes that should not be missed.

Once called to order, the agenda had to be formalized—is that "new business" or "old?"—then the minutes of the previous meeting read and approved and the date of the next meeting quibbled over and finally scheduled. An extensive discussion followed, something about the allocation of a "transient bed tax." The tax, he learned, had originally been imposed to raise money for tourist and information offices "just like this one," but much of the revenue was now being funneled into the county's general fund "where it promptly disappeared." A letter had to be written. Their elected supervisor approached. Responsibilities assigned. Motions were made, seconded, discussed and approved.

At long last the members arrived at the new business portion of the agenda and the subject of a mural to be placed on the wall of an adjoining building. Turghoff passed copies of the sketch around. For the benefit of the small audience, he set one on an easel that he had hauled in for the occasion. As he turned back toward his chair, he bumped the easel which crashed into a rack of brochures causing the sketch, the easel, the rack and a waterfall of brochures to cascade to the floor where they quickly spread themselves under the table and around the feet of the board members.

In time, all items, aside from a few stepped-upon and mutilated brochures, were returned to their intended positions, and Turghoff took his seat and gathered in a long, slow breath.

A board member wanted to know exactly what wall he was talking about. Turghoff explained which wall. Someone suggested they go out and look at the wall. That proposal was put off until later, perhaps for fear of another disaster should Turghoff again rise to his feet.

How large would the mural be? Turghoff explained the size. "That big?" Yes, that big. It was a mural not a painting. The proposal was to cover a large section of wall with the image the members had before them. The idea was to command attention. Catch the eyes of passersby and thereby draw tourists into the facility in which they were now sitting.

Heads nodded. Compliments were paid to the sketch. Emboldened, Turghoff launched into his rap about community participation, school children, social and service organizations, the branding of the community as a place known for its attractive, informative murals. He had assumed, after his presentation to the chamber and Yvonne's three published articles, that all of this would be common knowledge, but apparently none of it was. "Well, that's a wonderful idea," one member exclaimed as if he, Turghoff, were expressing it for the first time.

The board, after considerable discussion, appeared excited about the mural and its proposed location, though one member, a woman Turghoff had not met before, claimed that the clothing worn by the native man in his sketch was not authentic. Or if it was authentic somewhere, it was not authentic to the local native bands.

She was a thin woman in her fifties with watery blue eyes. A pair of reading glasses hung from her neck. Her earrings and necklace were beaded. Her long hair, it seemed to him, clung to its blondeness only with chemical assistance. She managed one of the motels near the interchange at the western end of town.

"The last thing we want to do is offend," she said. And the way she said it, her tone soft and apologetic, suggested that even uttering the word "offend" might itself be offensive.

Around the table heads nodded.

Turghoff explained that he had studied several early photographs and drawings. The clothing in his sketch, he said, was based, in large part, on a drawing made by an early settler in the community, a minister.

The woman scoffed at the idea that a minister could possibly have drawn an accurate portrait of a native man. The minister had obviously come to the area to Christianize the indigenous people and in so doing destroy their culture. She was surprised he had not depicted the poor fellow in an ill-fitting suit with "a Bible in his hand."

Howard Piggott, the burly owner of the antique store, a notary public and the informal mayor of the unincorporated village, who in his advanced years cruised the town in a dangerously high-powered wheelchair and attended every meeting he could find, had arrived moments earlier like a jousting knight on a dark horse and was now parked in the doorway. In a loud gravelly voice, Howard Piggott stated that he doubted that there remained any native people to be offended.

"I thought they'd all been killed off years ago," he concluded with what could have been interpreted as callous enthusiasm.

The hushed silence was broken by Jim Franklin's red suspenders, which, having been plucked like harp strings, slapped loud against Jim's firm, well-rounded belly. "Was disease that got 'em, Howard. That and the booze. My daddy used to talk about it. Diggers they were."

A gasp burst from the beaded woman and then more silence and finally a muttered exchange among the board members. No one seemed to know for sure if there existed any individuals in the community whose ancestors had been indigenous to the area. But as the beaded woman pointed out, this mural would be seen by thousands of people, not just locals, and it had to be as authentic as possible.

"I have some native blood myself," she announced, "but it is not local. So, I would not presume to speak for those who are."

"There must be a way to authenticate the clothing," a second board member mused. "Perhaps at the university? They have a Native American Studies department, don't they?"

"I think so," a third said. Around the table heads gave hesitant nods.

"Well, I guess I could check it out and get back to you," Turghoff suggested after a pause. He glanced helplessly at Yvonne, one of six audience members sitting on folding chairs near the door. And it seemed to him just then, that she looked both competent and stunning with a navy-blue baseball cap on her head, a splash of dark hair curling out the back, the spiral notebook resting open on a jean-covered thigh.

"It's not the job of a reporter to make suggestions," she said by way of introducing her suggestion, "but it might be helpful to Mr. Turghoff, if the board could, in the meantime, draft a letter that approves the mural and its proposed location, at least in concept. With the letter in hand he could approach the owner of the building about using the wall space."

It was getting close to lunch. Terry Clark, a ponytailed board member, the owner of the town's struggling book-store, and a friend of Turghoff's, said with sudden authority, "I so move."

The language of the letter was quibbled over, Yvonne making some suggestions, words of proper native dress inserted, and after the text had been read aloud from top to bottom, it was finally moved and adopted. Soon thereafter a motion to adjourn was approved.

CHAPTER SEVENTEEN

The next morning while frying eggs in a pool of splattering bacon fat, Robert Turghoff decided to invite the Curtiss family for dinner.

His desire for Yvonne continued to trouble him. Thoughts of her roiled his sleep, his leisurely swims, his dips in the spa. She had colonized his spirit and would not leave him alone. It was discomforting, almost demeaning, but—and here was the thing—it energized his work. Alone at night in the studio, his spirit had begun to sing again as it passed through his hands and brushes and onto the canvas.

It seemed to him now that in the last several years, his work, indeed, his life, had become mundane. He produced paintings. Galleries accepted his work. A couple times a year he traveled to cities as far removed as New York, Chicago and Bethesda to attend openings. Customers came. They viewed his work; they met and chatted with him, and some few bought paintings. Other orders came directly through his website, requiring him to roll prints into cardboard cylinders and deliver them to the post office. He wasn't getting rich. He was not a celebrity. But he had a reputation. He was dependable. He made a modest living, supplemented as needed by the plants out back.

But the paintings he had made over the last few years seemed now stale to him. They had not been copies but they were variations on familiar themes. He had become a specialist, turning out a known, recognizable product, a big-city surgeon who did several knee replacements each day, and nothing but knee replacements. Each painting, like each knee, was unique. It had its own features and challenges that had to be addressed, but the end result was always another knee.

But since Yvonne showed up with her notebook and her mischievous, troubled, not-quite- knowable temperament, new images started springing into his mind. As he walked the Big Hill trails, or swam, or cut firewood, images jumped out at him. And late at night alone in the studio with Jocko asleep in a chair, he painted those images, images that had nothing to do with Yvonne but came to life because of her.

A few years ago, a woman in Chicago who had purchased one of his pieces distinguished between "wilderness" and "wildness." It had been a brief conversation in a crowded gallery. He did not even remember her name, but what she said came back to him now. Ansel Adams's timeless photographs or Peter Holbrook's stunning landscapes, she told him, portrayed the magnificence of wilderness. "But your work in some intimate way reveals nature's 'wildness.'"

Yes, that was what he was after. Intimate visions of nature close up and untouched: new growth and old, reckless, spontaneous, fragile, resilient, damaged as life damages, beautiful, brutal and innocent, the force of nature more than the image itself. Three curly docks gone rusty and tilted; five intricate exploding teasels; stalks of windblown grasses in their seasons; a branch of oak, dense and muscular, dark with leaves or bare of them with knobby protrusions and stark angles; a cluster of mistletoe hung high on a branch; Queen Anne's Lace, lovely in bloom or fisted and seed-forming; the greens and yellows of fennel grown gangly with flowers; the ghost-like stalks of spent hemlock in winter. The results were not landscapes. He was in thrall of the isolated image, the angle, the shape, the voluptuous filling of a space. He set the images against flat mono-colored backgrounds almost as if they had been stenciled on a wall. The paintings possessed power, it seemed to him, tension, vitality.

And he was not alone. He posted images of a few on his website and the responses were encouraging. Calls came in, emails. Ben and David at the Haut Gallery in Chicago ordered two of the new paintings. They already had a collector who was interested.

Yvonne had become his muse, and was thus integral to his present being. Who he was now included Yvonne, but he knew the situation was unsustainable. Sooner or later bad things would happen. To trip blithely along whistling a happy tune was madness.

His was a mind in turmoil. The large man in the propane truck tugged at his imagination. Gil Curtiss had become a gravitational force orbiting out of view. Until he met the husband, until he drank a beer with the man, until they shot the shit as they walked around his property, Gil's existence had no grounding for him.

Turghoff needed to make a personal assessment. He wanted to stand close to Gil Curtiss, hear his voice, his laugh, follow his thinking, measure his height and weight, catch a whiff of his sweat, watch how his eyes held or flitted about, study his hands, the tension in his neck and shoulders. Would he discover a sweet, innocent fellow who fished and drove a propane truck and loved his wife and daughter, a large tail-wagging, house-dog kind of husband? Or would he find a ruined warrior with an edge of suspicion, anger, even hostility? What, if anything, had Yvonne told Gil about him? Or Carly? Had she spoken of Mom's friend the painter? Was Gil curious, suspicious? Did he already know? And if not, how would he behave when he did?

As even a beautiful melody tilts toward its resolution, so Turghoff's life, though exciting, productive and lust-rich, leaned now toward accommodation. He wanted a configuration that allowed him to retain the inspiration while the tension subsided. He would ease himself into the Curtiss family. He would become part of it the way he was a part of the Solomon family. He and the Solomons were close, they spent time together, had a shared history, but he had no designs on Patty. And so it could be here. He liked Carly; he felt a kinship with her artistic turn of mind. Maybe he and Gil could fish the river—catch and release it was now—or run over to the coast one low-tide morning and harvest some mussels. In his fantasy he would step gracefully back from the affair with Yvonne while somehow preserving the creative energy it gave him.

Then Turghoff found himself entertaining a stunning idea. He would extend the dinner invitation to the Solomons as well. The idea was inspired, it seemed to him. The two girls were friends, Patty and Yvonne were friends. He and Solomon and Gil could hang out on the back porch, beers in hand, salmon steaks on the grill. Tension would be scattered and weakened.

So, first steps first. At the very least get to know the players. And in this game Gil Curtiss was one of the players. He may, Turghoff realized, even be the captain. So, yes, he would invite them to dinner. If Yvonne resisted, he would push the idea.

§

Patty Solomon was not enthused about his proposed dinner. "You want to invite our family to your house for the sole purpose of enticing her family there, so you can catch an unguarded look at her husband? Isn't that what they call chumming?"

"Chumming?" Turghoff was confused.

"Yes, I believe that's the word. We have a client who brags about it. An elderly fellow who always wears suspenders and those blue and white striped logging shirts. The old wide kind of suspenders that attach with buttons, not clips. This gentleman chums, he tells me. He's quite proud of how he never has to leave home to get his buck. He just scatters a few apples around the backyard, sits on the porch with his rifle and waits."

"It is not my intent to shoot Yvonne's husband, Patty, if that's what you're implying. I thought I mentioned a social evening. The two girls together, the five of us. Salmon on the grill, corn on the cob. We talk, we share histories, gossip. I even hoped you might volunteer a bowl of your well-known potato salad."

"I see. And Yvonne? What has she offered to contribute?"

Turghoff thought he discerned a trace of irony lining the Boss's refined voice. She probably knew more about the Curtiss family's domestic life than he did. But he had not yet suggested the dinner to Yvonne. He wanted to know first that the Solomons were coming. "I thought maybe some dip and a bag or two of chips. I'm reluctant to suggest she actually prepare a dish. You probably know more than I do, but I suspect they pretty much subsist on takeout and generic frozen entrees." He paused before adding: "And on one occasion at least, raw liver."

That caught Patty's attention, though she captured her surprise before it escaped her lips. After which she nodded her head slowly. "The native thing."

"You've heard."

124

"A vague reference, nothing more."

"There's a movie I understand that Gil loves. He watches it all the time."

"The movie I haven't heard about."

"Well, there's a buffalo hunt. And when the buffalo is killed, the braves slice the carcass open. They pull out the liver; they pass it around and everyone takes a bite. So, one night, Gil..."

"You may spare me the details," Patty said, grimacing.

Turghoff nodded. Beef tartare Patty might try, were it paired with the correct wine as instructed by her well-schooled husband. Given the occasion she might dare a raw oyster on the half shell. And he knew the Solomons had the gadgets needed to roll their own sushi. But buffalo liver still warm from the body consumed while standing on the high plains, or raw beef liver sampled on the living room couch, was more than she was prepared to contemplate. And he as well, for that matter.

"I thought we could put Solly in charge of the wine selection. Nothing fancy. Something white, of course, with the salmon. But he will know."

"When it comes to wine, Robert, Solly doesn't do 'nothing fancy' anymore. It's become a sort of obsession, I'm afraid. He recently completed a weekend tasting course at UC Davis, and came back enthused. There will be an aperitif of some sort, something bubbly perhaps, or a rosé, then probably three different whites, a sauvignon blanc, a couple of chardon-nays differing slightly in sweetness and varying trace elements;

following the meal an aged port. If we're outside he might even produce cigars for you gentlemen. But that presents a problem, does it not?"

"A problem?"

"I'm reluctant to betray a confidence, but it seems unavoidable. Are you unaware that Gil's an alcoholic?"

"Christ! No, I mean yes, I had just forgotten." Turghoff slapped his hands against the sides of his head. He could picture it: Solomon, Patty, he and Yvonne seated at his battered picnic table glowing and giggling from fermented grape juice while enthusing about the "legs" in their glasses and the hints of vanilla and pineapple, while Gil sat alone struggling to imagine himself in a sweat lodge. Not the evening he had hoped for. "All I'm trying to do, Patty, is create a fucking mural in the center of town."

His daughter's former babysitter offered a sly smile. "Let's be honest, Robert. That's not exactly true, is it? The mural is not the only thing going on here."

CHAPTER EIGHTEEN

When Turghoff heard the mail drop daily through the slot, which usually happened in late morning about the time he was waking up, he often thought of his son Vince. Vince was fifteen when Jen and the kids left, and Marta turned twelve in Colorado a few weeks later. Marta and he talked on the phone, though that had been less frequent now that she was beginning college. But she was active on social media where Turghoff caught glimpses of her developing life and her passion for soccer.

Vince wanted nothing to do with electronics; he even claimed to hate computers though he had to use one constantly. He also hated cars, airplanes and electric guitars. He did not call or email and had no presence on social media. Vince believed that he (and everyone else) was being watched by silent, endlessly operating algorithms. So, he kept in touch with his father through hand-written letters, which he signed not with his name but with an instruction as if his letter were a problem: Solve for V. Shortly after the family broke up Vince had mailed him a single sheet of paper that contained the following message: (J+R+V+M)>(J+V+M-R), which Turghoff treasured and kept taped on a wall in the breakfast nook.

Vince believed himself born in the wrong century. "I would have been better off hanging out with George Boole," he wrote, which sent Turghoff to Wikipedia where he met an obscure 19th century English mathematician. Somehow his son had managed to earn a bachelor's degree in mathematics and was now a teaching assistant and working toward a master's at Florida State.

So, they had exchanged hand-written letters from the beginning. Turghoff never succumbed to the temptation to remind his son that their letters were written on paper produced from fallen trees mashed up with toxic chemicals in foul-smelling paper mills and transported by trucks and planes, and were thus as damaging to the planet as the electricity-sucking internet. He was just happy to get the letters and to hear in his mind the sound of his son's voice as he read them.

Vince's letters were often hilarious with notes jotted on the outside of the envelope presumably to entertain bored postal employees as well as Turghoff. But the letters came less frequently now and Vince's focus seemed ever tighter, more obscure. He appeared to be organizing his world into sets and sets within sets, his beautiful blue-inked script broken by parentheses and brackets and parentheses within brackets. The content was disjointed and at times incoherent, at least to him, though he realized that others might recognize it as brilliant. Sometimes now, when he woke to the sound of the mail being delivered, Turghoff realized he had been dreaming about his son. The dreams were discomforting. His son retching in a dark alley, or his body being lowered into the ground and Turghoff arriving late having missed both the death and the funeral.

§

The call came on a Thursday that the grapes were ready, and moments later Solomon was on the phone, excited. The vineyard would be harvested the next day. They were to be at the site by eight. They could choose the row they wanted and help with the harvest. Bring your own container, he had been told, and a truck to haul it in. The container would be weighed empty and again loaded and the owner wanted cash. No credit cards, no debit cards, no checks. Cash.

From somewhere Solomon had borrowed two half-ton plastic, macro-bins. Empty they weighed about a hundred pounds each. Together, Solomon said, he and Turghoff could muscle them onto the bed of Old Ugly, Turghoff's pickup.

And full, Turghoff wanted to know.

Solomon had a patient who was the foreman at the lumberyard. He would bring a forklift to Solomon's place to unload them.

The bins could stand a forklift?

They're built for it, Solomon told him. But they had to be at the vineyard by eight. Patty was on the phone cancelling and rescheduling his Friday appointments.

Turghoff, following a mental map, walked into the orchard behind the studio where he unearthed a jar of rolled bills. A few rolls he threw in the glove compartment. They were on the road by five.

They rumbled down 101, the macro-bins jostling empty in the truck bed, music emerging from static to clarity and receding again as radio signals strengthened and weakened. It was a cool morning with a broken sky but they kept the windows cracked open to dilute the exhaust fumes making their way into the cab.

Solomon was rattling on about "must" and "yeast," about "fermentation" and "tannic acid." He was forecasting a busy weekend, picking through the grapes, tossing out the stems and spoiled fruit and getting the good stuff into the fermenter. His daughter Britt had promised to help and maybe she could snare one or two of her friends.

Turghoff liked the idea. "It'll be like a peasant village at harvest time. We'll crush the grapes with our feet!"

Solomon looked vaguely nauseous. "Sorry, with pinot we don't crush. Not until later. The grapes go whole into the fermenter. And it has to be very sanitary. But Patty will devil eggs and cut slices of salami and cook pasta and throw salads together. We'll pull a cork or two as the day goes on."

As if offering a toast, Turghoff raised the luke-warm four-shot latte from its warm snuggle at his crotch and took a sip.

It was not his time of day and he needed the caffeine to keep his mind on the road. His plan had been to skip his usual night of studio work and sleep through. He had forced himself to stay awake until eleven by watching his much-treasured, never-loaned-out VHS copy of "The Horse's Mouth" with Alec Guinness. But then at one o'clock, while snug in bed, the room dark, the house quiet, he came fully awake. It was as if his body realized, even if he did not, that the food that kept it alive, the shelter that kept it warm and dry, all resulted from Turghoff being in the studio most of the night, paintbrush in hand.

In the noisy truck, Solomon was orating about hydrometers and titration and pH levels, about first and second fermentations, about new and used oak barrels and a thing called "racking," which apparently had nothing to do with torture.

Meanwhile Turghoff was back in bed trying to decide what to do. If he got up and went to the studio he would never get any rest. He was supposed to pick up Solomon at five. He had set the alarm for four-thirty, and had already resigned himself to a few bites of granola rather than the usual eggs and bacon. But in the studio his painter personality would take full control and he would find himself wide awake until the hour the alarm was set to go off. At which point his dear and faithful corpus would imagine itself back on the mattress for that sweetest of all rests, the work-completed morning snooze—just as he was about to begin a long and taxing day.

In his early twenties, maybe. Today no. So, he had not gone to the studio. He had stayed in the bed, opened and closed his eyes, tried different positions, commanded his body to relax as if it were a pet or a child. He checked and rechecked the alarm. He attempted to follow his breathing. He counted sheep and deliberately did not look at the clock. He tried to imagine again that beach on Kauai where he and Jen had made love that time and where they both felt that they had joined sperm and egg and begun the existence of Vince. But thoughts of his children probed old wounds and suggested new worries. What was happening with Vince? He should call Jen and get her take.

"These are going to be high quality grapes," Solomon was saying. "And not just that, they are pinot, the most noble of wine grapes. We need to approach this project with all the respect due them. Yes, we can have fun. Yes, it will be a party. But we have to be precise. We must be careful with our measurements and calculations, and above all we must adopt and adhere to good sanitary practices."

Solomon was soon onto yeast starter and Campden tablets and bottles and the used floor-standing bottle corker he had picked up for next to nothing and that worked perfectly.

"*Our* yeast is *our* champion," Solomon shouted above the music and the wind whistling through the windows and Old Ugly's cacophony of rattles. "All others will be denied. Only our yeast will be free to feed and flourish in the must. No leaves, no stems, no radical bacteria from feet or hands, just *our* yeast!"

Turghoff felt honored to be in the company of such enthusiasm. He was waking and starting to feel invigorated. This was my Solomon, he thought. Whether he was pounding boards together, or cracking backs or wooing his lovely English lass, Solomon had always preserved and given voice to the romantic poet hidden in the recesses of his personality.

CHAPTER NINETEEN

At the vineyard there must have been fifteen or more friendly dark-eyed Hispanic guys in work shirts and loose-fitting jeans; baseball caps on their heads, some bills fore, others aft. With quick hands and sturdy backs they had the allotment picked and the bins loaded in less than half an hour. He and Solomon had brought shears and gloves, thinking they would help with the harvest, but they were like a couple of middle-aged guys in gym gear walking onto the floor of an NBA game hoping to play. They had hardly selected their row when the task was finished. All they could manage was to toss aside the occasional leaf that landed in a bin. That and of course put down the cash.

The grapes themselves were astonishingly beautiful. Not black, as he had assumed, but large, sky-blue, wonderfully spherical and succulent. The dense, heavy bunches, thick and wide at the top narrowed down to a tip. Held aloft by a severed stem they appeared continent-shaped: Africa, perhaps, or South America. Their fullness suggested fertility and warmth. Solomon was right: singularly, or bunched, or massed in the bins, they evoked nobility and wealth.

Solomon wanted to leave immediately but Turghoff insisted on taking a few photos to record his impressions should he ever want to paint the images he saw around him. But the most powerful sensations—the shears snipping like feeding insects, the men rushing, their occasional bursts of Spanish, their internal camaraderie and playful competition, the pungent smells of earth, of plants and fruit as the vineyard warmed in the sun—all that lay outside the camera's frame.

On the drive back Solomon took the wheel of the heavy-laden truck and Turghoff enjoyed a half-hour nap. At Willits, the truck visible and parked in the shade, they had lunch, and Turghoff brought up the subject that had been on his mind since early morning.

"Do you know Gil Curtiss?" he asked.

Solomon had been slightly annoyed about stopping for lunch. His mind was on the making of wine and the precious cargo they were transporting. When Turghoff woke and mentioned lunch, Solomon had said, "You know, don't you, that making pinot is a very tricky business. That is not just a bunch of grapes back there; it's not like merlot or something. Those are pinot grapes back there.

"We have bought our way into a high-stakes game, Turghoff, and the partner we're playing with is a spoiled bastard. Pinot is a spoiled bastard, a characteristic that comes from its nobility. There is nothing workaday or plebeian about this grape. Even if we do everything right, the wine might still turn out to be shit. It has its own mind, pinot does. If it agrees to like you it goes along. If not, it gets pissy." Solomon seemed to be suggesting that making wine and having lunch were in some way incompatible.

But now, seated at the restaurant table, he sighed and slowly shook his head.

"Does that mean you don't know Gil Curtiss?" Turghoff asked.

"Are you still into that?"

"I'm asking you a simple question. Do you know Gil Curtiss?"

"He's a guy drives a truck for NewFuel. Every six months or so he stops by and tops off our tank."

Turghoff had the impression that Solomon was experiencing buyer's remorse. They had acquired a ton of expensive grapes and all he saw ahead of him was hours of work and the distinct likelihood of disaster. Two barrels of disaster, which is to say three hundred bottles of bad wine for each of them. It could make for several dark and dreary winters. Turghoff had been blessed with a peasant's palate but poor Solomon, he could taste the subtleties.

"I've met him," Solomon finally acknowledged. "I've seen him at school functions, I've been by their place to pick up

Britt. Patty has had more contact than I have. And she's talked to me. So, you are getting into this deeper and deeper."

It was not a question. The tone more resembled a judge handing down a sentence. When Turghoff first met Solomon, the carpenter had a black beard and dense curly hair. He wore a red bandana across his forehead like an Apache warrior, had black leather straps on his wrists, and he seemed possessed of an irrepressible, mischievous mirth, an aspect of personality well suited to those who spend their days converting hard, resistant materials into objects of use and functional beauty. Now the beard was gone. Patty ran an electric clippers over his head once a week leaving a black stubble flecked with gray the uniform length of half an inch or so. The leather straps had disappeared years ago. On his left wrist hung a gold watch more ostentatious than practical. And from his mouth came gloom and doom. Well, Turghoff conceded, he does devote himself to people in pain, always knowing there are limits to what he can do to help. Over time that would have to shape you in some way.

"What's your impression of him?"

Their food had come. Solomon had ordered a Reuben and a cup of coffee and the waitress forgot to bring the coffee and he reminded her and when she still did not bring it he went over to the counter and told her again.

The coffee finally arrived. Solomon lifted the top slice of rye and studied the internal ingredients of his sandwich with a suspicious look. He put the slice back in place and said,

"This is not a good idea. What you are getting into is going to end badly."

"Tell me what you can," Turghoff said, his mouth half full of a BLT. "I'm not asking you to violate any confidences, if he's your patient."

"He is not my patient, she is," Solomon said.

"Oh."

"He's pleasant enough, though he avoids a direct look. He's been through hell and may be crazy, or at least have that predilection. And he's probably a drunk, though I understand he's doing the twelve-step dance at the moment. And he's the stable one in the family."

"He's…?"

Solomon nodded.

"She's…?"

"I can't talk about her."

"No, I just didn't know she was a patient of yours." Turghoff felt a jealous pang knowing that Solomon had run his hands over Yvonne's body.

They chewed. Solomon kept looking out at the truck.

"I don't understand," Turghoff finally said. "About the husband. You say he's crazy and a drunk…"

"I want to get those grapes indoors."

"So, how's he land a job driving a truck loaded with propane? That's like driving around with a bomb, isn't it? Aren't there requirements?"

"Daddy."

"Daddy? His daddy...?"

"Her daddy," Solomon said. "Daddy owns the company, or at least part of it. My guess: Daddy wanted to get them out of Santa Rosa so he wrangled the job for him up here. Greased a few gears. There were problems down there. And you know, it's every parent's lament: they got in with the wrong crowd. So, get them out of town. Give them a fresh start."

"Yes."

Solomon wrapped the remains of his Reuben in a paper napkin; he downed the last of his coffee and stood up. "Those grapes are my children. I want them home before any harm comes to them."

"Yes." Turghoff pushed himself back from the table. He grabbed the crust of his sandwich and stuffed it into his mouth.

CHAPTER TWENTY

Turghoff hoped Patty and Solly would invite the Curtiss family to what Solomon was calling the "vine-to-wine" party. It would be a perfect way for him to casually meet Gil Curtiss. Four adults and four children were present when Turghoff arrived, including two girlfriends of Britt's, neither of whom Turghoff knew. Montoya the plumber was there along with Headlong who brought his usual intensity but not much staying power. The Curtiss family did not appear. They had not been invited, he finally realized, because *he* was. He had become a contaminant, a toxic agent best kept free of Yvonne and her husband, at least in the eyes of his good friends the Solomons.

The purpose of "vine to wine" was to separate all worthy grapes from their stems and other debris and deliver them safely into the fermenter. Solomon insisted on strenuous hand-washing by everyone who intended to touch the fruit. As they were pulled free, the grapes had to be examined by Solomon who peered into the soul of each to certify that it possessed not mold nor fungus nor lack of moisture. Within an hour the kids had lost interest and were playing badminton in the backyard. Montoya had cracked a beer, Turghoff held a deviled egg in a grape-stained hand and Solomon was rubbing his eyes. A ton of grapes turned out to be a lot of grapes.

It was almost dark when the last of the selected fruit had been carefully placed in the fermenter. Then, like an officiating priest, Solomon added the precious yeast and, spreading his arms wide, announced: "Let the magic begin!"

§

Back at the house Turghoff found Yvonne parked in her open convertible, smoking a cigarette. It was the first time he had seen her with a cigarette, though he had caught hints of smoke on her breath. From the beginning she had evoked for him a dangerous volatility that both repelled and attracted him, and seeing the cigarette tip glowing in the late light heightened his sense of unease. He had stopped smoking twenty years before. Now he masked his desire to bum one by reminding her of the dry grass and the risk her cigarette presented. The remark came off even to him as parental.

"Nice to see you, too," Yvonne muttered as she smashed the cigarette in the ashtray and got out of the car.

"You haven't been in this country long," he persisted. "There's a danger, that's all. Once you've seen a wildfire you will never forget it."

"I'm a California girl, Turghoff. I know about fire. Besides, I get enough of that at home."

Which home, he wondered. Her present one, or the one where she had grown up. He decided to not explore the details. They were two adults, attracted to each other sexually. There was nothing more, he told himself, and nothing less. Which meant that her demons were her business, not his and he needed to keep it that way. A breeze had come up as the sun set and the air smelled faintly of the dying cigarette and the pennyroyal her tires had crushed. The motion-sensitive yard light that had come on when he drove in flicked off with a click.

First stars appearing. Venus bright and sinking in the west. He was tired, flat from Patty's food and Solomon's wine. "Come with me," he said, as he led her into the house. "I want to show you something, Something I have not shown you before."

§

Moments later she sat up to her shoulders in hot water facing him. She was smiling now and Turghoff thought himself a lucky man.

A few months after he and Alicia bought the property Turghoff had installed a hot tub off the bedroom. It had been part of his desperate struggle to keep his first wife comfortable and their marriage viable. Alicia said she liked the house but hated the temperature range not to mention the fumes and inconvenience of wood heat. She wanted a thermostat-controlled central heating system. Turghoff insisted they could not afford one (though secretly he preferred the wood heat) so he had put in the hot tub instead. Alicia loved the tub but one cannot stay in a hot tub all day; less than a year later she was on her way back to Boston and the urban life that called to her.

Jen, wife two, always claimed to be indifferent about the hot tub, though it was accepted doctrine that Marta had been conceived there on a moonless night, the Big Dipper pointing toward the North Star invisible beyond the roofline of the house.

One flush-feeling winter during his time with Jen, Turghoff sold off the redwood tub. He installed a gleaming, chocolate-colored, acrylic-skinned spa with foaming jets, which he surrounded with plank flooring, with windowless walls and with benches against the walls, and a closet space with hooks to hang clothing and robes. But the space above he had left open to the sky and the weather and the occasional smear of the Milky Way. The floor planking he had carefully sanded and periodically shellacked but the walls and benches remained raw, rough-cut and weathered. He loved the space.

Occasionally during his years with Jen the whole family would climb in and splash around with the water churning and yellow rubber ducks bobbing about. He remembered those evenings fondly, though in retrospect he suspected that his memories were fonder than those of Jen, Vince and Marta. He and

Jen often bickered whether in the house or in the spa, he now remembered, and the kids argued; often the three of them would return to the house and he would be left alone in the water.

Hung off the woodsy rear of the house, the spa was virtually unnoticeable, its only access being through his bedroom. If the studio was where his artist's heart lived, and the pool and living room his welcoming venues, the spa was his private and personal refuge. Most visitors never knew of its existence. Yvonne herself had not known of it until now.

"I feel betrayed, Turghoff. You fucked me in the pool. You fucked me that time on the arm of that terrible chair in the studio, though only God knows how we did that without breaking something. And you fucked me in your bed. But until this evening, you had never shown me this place, even hinted at its existence."

The instep of her foot grazed against the inside of his calf. The jets turned themselves off and the room quieted. Turghoff felt flat, drowsy. Evening air descended from the open roof and settled around them.

"Until now," he said, his hands lightly stroking the hot water.

"Exactly."

"You are a mystery to me and I wanted to know you better before I brought you out here."

"So now you think you know me, huh?"

He shrugged. "Enough to risk it, I suppose. But you do puzzle me. Take that indigo convertible, for example. The expensive clothes, the dangling silver trinkets. Meanwhile you talk of debt and desperation. That puzzles me."

For reasons unclear to him he felt a cold pleasure as he uttered those words. Yvonne moved her legs away from his; her lovely breasts dripped water as she pushed herself higher in the seat. He sensed an abrupt shift of mood, as if he had changed their conversation from teasing chatter to interrogation.

"The Miata Roadster was a gift my husband gave me when he was finally discharged from the army. He insisted on it because he regretted joining and he knew what his joining had put me through. I know that sounds twisted considering what he went through, but it's the truth."

"Okay."

"Of course he had no money to buy the car beyond the minimal down payment and he was suckered into the deal by some predatory lender who said he could offer a loan available only to veterans. Six months or something with no interest."

"Okay," Turghoff said again.

"No *payments* for six months, he should have said. Interest was piling up all the while. The car is as underwater as you and I are sitting here. Or were." Yvonne pushed herself out of the water and stood dripping on the deck. "If you have no further questions I will be on my way."

"Yvonne…"

She wrapped herself in a towel, gathered up her clothes and disappeared into his bedroom slamming the door behind her.

Turghoff sank under the water, and he blew out some air before pushing himself up again. His fate, it seemed, was to be left in hot water while those he loved had in discontent departed.

In the half-hour soak that followed he came to realize that Yvonne's use of the word "fuck" to describe sexual intercourse had troubled him. No woman he knew spoke that way. Women said so and so were "sleeping together," as if they were describing a couple who rented a motel room, locked the door, ripped each-others clothes off and promptly collapsed on the bed snoring.

But she had said he "fucked" her. He fucked her in the pool, fucked her in the studio, fucked her in the bed. Not something they did together; something he did to her. The word implied brutality to him, perhaps violence. He found it shocking, arousing in some way, but the crudeness had misled him. He suspected now that Yvonne had used the word to hide a deeper truth: she felt vulnerable in the world, a raw nerve being jabbed at by his questions.

She did not return to the spa, as he hoped she might, and by the time he left for the bedroom he had decided to order flowers sent to her. To the office of *The Woeful* with some innocuous note of thanks for help with the mural.

CHAPTER TWENTY-ONE

Carly had started coming to the studio. She stopped by two afternoons before the trip to the vineyard. First on a Thursday, and then again the following Tuesday. She came alone and he thought it brave of her to just show up like that.

The first visit found him stacking firewood against the wall behind the stove in the studio, and she helped by carrying in a few armfuls. Then a short time later she left suddenly as if she had gotten embarrassed, as if she had asked herself what she was doing there. Or maybe his behavior made her think she was intruding and unwelcome. He told her she did not have to rush off, but, no, she said she had to go and turned and walked down the drive to the road.

He saw something hesitant and fragile about her as she walked away. What was the pack doing on her back? School was not in session. He kicked himself for not asking if she had brought drawings. Or a snack? A bottle of water? He realized that he did not know where the Curtiss family lived or how far she had to walk to get home. Maybe he should have offered to drive her. He had just stood there and as she walked down the drive he thought she would never come back. The feeling was like when you come upon a wild animal and it looks at you for a moment, curious, and then turns and trots away. Only this had not been a wild animal. This had been Carly Curtiss, the girl everyone said needed help.

But then the next Tuesday she showed up again. That was the afternoon he decided to finally cut back the grasses and thistles that had grown up around the house and studio. They were fully dried and ready fuel for the flick of an ash or the touch of a hot catalytic converter hanging below a car. He was locked inside goggles and ear-protectors, his gloved hands gripping a roaring weedwacker when she arrived. It was not until he stopped to refuel that he saw her watching him from a few feet away.

She had been there only a couple of minutes, she said, though he was not sure he believed her. Her disappointment was obvious and this time he understood. He was a painter and she wanted to see him paint. Why wasn't he painting?

"I paint while you sleep," he told her, "but I'll show you what I'm working on."

The night before he had started preparing a new painting. The canvas was good size, rectangular, wider than tall and he had undercoated the entire surface a smooth sky-blue. He showed her the canvas and then directed her attention to some photographs tacked on the wall.

"These are not art," he said to her. "The photographs aren't intended as art. I took them to aid my memory, the way your mom takes notes at a meeting so she has the information when she writes an article. My goal is not to paint what you see in the photographs, not exactly. I took them several years ago, and the other night I remembered them. I don't know why, I just remembered that afternoon, and I printed a few of the photographs and tacked them up here."

The photographs were set at his eye level, too high for her to see well. He considered lifting her by the waist but then thought better of it. He pulled over a chair and had her climb up.

"I was charmed by what I saw that day," he explained. "It was a sunny January afternoon and I was walking along an old logging road. The road had been cut into the side of a hill. It's not visible in the photos but below and to my left was the river. It was after a heavy rain, and the river was high and fast-flowing. The road's not far from here. I could take you there sometime."

"My dad might walk there," Carly said. "He goes for long walks. Sometimes it's after dark when he comes home."

"Alone?"

"Yes, he likes to be alone."

So, Turghoff had another image: a large man yelling from behind the wheel of a propane truck, a man naked in a bathtub holding a pistol, a man alone walking down an abandoned logging road.

"Anyway, above on my right was the fairly steep bank that you see in this photo. It's raw dirt, kind of unstable-looking, don't you think?"

She nodded.

"It's hard to tell in the photos but those trees are well-above the bank, maybe ten, fifteen yards above where I was standing. It was winter like I said which is why the oaks have no leaves. The neat thing about deciduous trees is that in winter the bare branches are exposed. You can see their lumpy, muscular shapes and the abrupt and stunning angles they make at times. Like these. Look at these! I had the zoom on here. I wanted to get a better view of the branches."

"He brings things back for me," she said.

"Your dad?"

"If I'm in bed he puts them on the kitchen table and I find them in the morning."

"I see." He paused but she did not continue. "What I like about the trees themselves is their strength. Take this limb. See how far it is suspended out horizontal from the trunk? Think of the weight of it, the strength it takes to hold it there. Think what it would be like in a storm, or when it's covered in wet snow or thick with leaves and acorns, and everything is wet and the wind is howling."

"Like here?" She pointed toward a tree beyond the one his camera had focused on where a rough stub protruded from the trunk.

"Yes, exactly. A branch got ripped off from there somehow. A storm probably. If we climbed up the bank we might see it lying in the grass. Or maybe it rolled down and ended up on the road and somebody cut it up and took it home for firewood.

"That's what struck me at the time. How precarious it all was, how uncertain, and yet strong. How it was changing and yet staying the same. The road, the whole hillside is sort of suspended above the river. The ground in this country is very unstable, did you know that? Long ago it was ocean bottom. It has been getting pushed up for millions of years, but at the same time it is also eroding, sluffing off, sliding down.

"So, the trees are suspended above this unstable bank with their long, heavy limbs hanging from the trunks at odd and surprising angles. It's almost as if everything is falling toward the river. And really it is. Given enough time it will all end in the river and then back in the ocean. But from our perspective it isn't moving at all. Everything is in a state of suspension. It's precarious and yet stable, enduring and strong, very strong."

"What are those?" Carly asked, pointing.

Turghoff smiled. "Those are another subject of my painting."

"They look like giant Christmas balls."

"Yes, I think so too. That's mistletoe. The same plant some people hang over a door at Christmas time so it's not surprising they remind us of Christmas."

Carly had never heard of anyone hanging a twig of mistletoe over a doorway at Christmas time.

"It's an old tradition. If you meet someone you love under a doorway that has mistletoe over it, you are supposed to kiss them."

"Really?" Her expression suggested disgust. "You mean, like you have to?"

"I don't think it's required," Turghoff said. "It's just a tradition. Maybe people don't do it anymore." He directed her attention back to the blue canvas. 'So, we have this empty canvas. My idea is to paint a single limb, one of those strong bare ones, maybe the one with the angle, or maybe the angle will be too much. I'll make some sketches first to see. Anyway, I will definitely want some smaller branches coming off the limb. Not too many branches. I don't want the image to look cluttered, but I like the little branches. See how they form sharp angles jutting off from themselves? I like that. They make me think of claws maybe, or fangs."

"Or antlers, like from a deer," Carly suggested. "My dad brought me an antler once. I found it on the table. I still have it in my room. Another time I found the skin from a snake. I have it too. Mom didn't like that. Not on the table. She's worried till he comes back."

Turghoff nodded. "And hanging from the limb will be a single cluster of mistletoe. I'll choose one of the nice plump ones."

"If it gets dark," she continued. "And he's not back." She stared at the canvas. "So, where's the tree go?"

"The tree? Well, you won't see the tree. Not the trunk or the hillside. Just one limb that enters the frame with a few branches."

"That's all?"

"That's it, plus the mistletoe. The rest stays the color you see. But my goal is to imply everything we've talked about. The blue sky is obvious, but also the unseen stuff, the steep, unstable hillside, the trees supporting themselves up there, the strong heavy, hanging limbs. I want to suggest both the strength and the fragility that I saw on the hillside that day. All of that will be in the back of my mind as I paint. And one other thing. Something I haven't told you yet, but it's very important and we can't forget: the mistletoe plant is a parasite. That round and jolly cluster of leaves and stems is feeding off the tree. In time it will kill the limb, maybe the tree itself."

He stepped back and studied the canvas. Yes, that is what he wanted. He could see how it should be. He started to speak but Carly seemed to have lost interest. She was not looking at the canvas or apparently listening to him anymore.

"Why aren't these art?" she asked now pointing at the wall.

"What? The photographs?"

She nodded, and he was stunned for a moment. "If you become an artist, Carly, you will spend your lifetime thinking about that question. So, do they fight?"

"All the time," she said.

CHAPTER TWENTY-TWO

In the Solomons' driveway, Solomon was muttering to himself but Turghoff got the gist: "Very bad wine can be made from very good grapes. Especially pinot."

Solomon continued to mutter as he led them into the subterranean garage between the two parked cars and through a metal door to a room in the rear where the air possessed a fragrance and a damp coolness that Turghoff found refreshing. The fermenter stood against the back wall, and before the fermenter were the two wine barrels causing Solomon's despair.

"The wood is too dense and the grain's too fine. I was promised barrels of French oak and these are made of American oak. The guy's screwing me."

"So?" Turghoff wanted to know.

"So? So, we get bad wine, that's so. Merlot and Syrah are okay with either American or French. Apparently, Zin actually prefers American oak. But we have pinot and pinot must be aged in barrels made from the wood of oak trees grown in certain parts of France. And we don't have time to ship these back and order from another supplier. We're screwed."

"He's got us over a barrel all right." Turghoff started to laugh then stopped.

"Don't start that."

"Okay,"

"It's very technical, this thing with the barrels. And it's not just French or American. There are new barrels and used barrels, charred barrels and toasted barrels. On the other hand, some barrels are neither toasted nor charred." Solomon used his shoe to nudge the closest barrel and Turghoff had the impression that what he really wanted was to kick it.

"These barrels are used and toasted but not charred. Some say you should use new barrels, others used, some say toasted, others not. And that's just the barrels. At least these fuckers are used. New barrels import too much oak."

"Okay."

"He insists they're French, but I'm sure they're American! The more I know about this business the worse it gets. The other day I read an article online by a reputable winemaker who claimed that we should not have destemmed all the grapes, just most of them. Maybe ten, twenty percent we should have left in their clusters."

"Just throw whole bunches in the fermenter?"

"Some say more, some less, others do zero like we did. Stems, this guy claimed, enhance tannin and spicy flavors like vanilla, and they give the wine more body—but the stems must be hard and brown, not green. Were ours green or brown?"

"Both, I think."

"Anyway it's too late. The deed is done." Solomon scratched his burry head. "Then this morning I found an article on pinot that assumed no stems in the must and all the grapes had been crushed prior to fermentation."

"Crushed? You mean, like with our feet? The way I wanted?"

"Apparently. Some say crush a few, most say no. It's a mess. At least the yeast I used gets good reviews. Which is why I picked it. Supposed to provide a good nose, a fruity flavor and a complex profile. On the other hand, some suggest you add no cultured yeast at all. Just throw the whole mess in the fermenter, grapes and stems, your kid's baby shoes, and let nature take its course."

"Nature," Turghoff said.

"Good luck with that. But even so this fermentation thing has been a nightmare. I had to make sure the temperature of the must was above 12C but not above 24C. Too cold it stops, too high the whole process gets stuck. The stuff heats up, that's what fermentation does. I would wake up in the middle of the night thinking about the must, thinking it must be getting too hot. So I would run down here in my bare feet and stick in the thermometer. And I'd bring a plastic bag filled with ice."

"You threw ice in the must? Doesn't that water it down, the wine I mean?"

"No, no. I put the bag of ice in, not the ice itself. Then when the ice had melted I took the bag out. To lower the temperature."

"Okay."

"I only did that once. Sort of panicked. The temp was a little over 23C. But the other thing is the must separates. The cap, that's the solid stuff that forms on top, you know, the skins, the pulp. So twice a day I had to punch the cap down, mix it back in because the color comes from the skins. Otherwise you get a lousy color and who knows what else. And that process, punching it down, that had to be done without any contamination getting into the must. Everything that touches the must, must be sanitized."

Solomon sighed. He was obviously thinking about three hundred bottles of lousy wine.

"Well, at least it smells good down here," Turghoff offered, hoping to cheer up his friend.

"Britt says it stinks. She wants all the doors kept closed so the smell doesn't get upstairs. And when she wants to go somewhere she descends by the outside front steps and has me or Patty back the car out before she gets in."

"And Patty?"

"Patty is noncommittal on the whole subject. She may believe I have gone off the deep end, but she hasn't said that. Anyway, on the fifth day, I had to do the malolactic conversion."

"The…

"Malolactic conversion."

"Sounds like something dreamed up by the Vatican. You know those heathen malolactic people? Got to convert them." Turghoff hoped to elicit at least a smile. Instead he got a frown.

"Must develops malic acid, see, and malic acid tastes bad. So, I inoculated the must with a strain of bacteria that converts malic acid into lactic acid, which tastes better apparently. Of course some say this conversion happens naturally, but others say you can't count on that. With some wines you actually *want* malic acid. In that case you have to do something to prevent the natural conversion. But that's like Riesling or Gewürztraminer so we don't have to worry about that."

"Good."

"I did it on the fifth day, like I said, but some say it's better to do it later, after the wine is in the barrels."

"The conversion."

"Right. But then the problem is the temperature. It has to be the right temp for the conversion to happen, and controlling the temperature in the barrels…. So anyway, I decided it was better to convert now. You still with me?"

"Yes! And I get it. Nobody knows," Turghoff exclaimed. "That's what you're saying isn't it? All these experts, all these articles, and nobody knows. Everybody is winging it just like us. That should be of some relief, don't you think?"

"No! It's the exact opposite." Solomon was adamant. "Everybody knows but nobody agrees!"

"Everybody but us."

"Precisely. Everybody but us." And Solomon gave the barrel another kick.

§

But win, lose or draw, the time had come. According to Solomon's hydrometer the specific gravity of the must had fallen below1.00, which meant, he said, that what had been grape juice was now wine. Thus the time had come to apply the brakes, press it out, and rack it off.

"Brakes?"

Solomon pointed toward the fermenter. "There's an environmental disaster going on in there. As the yeast cells eat up the grapes they excrete alcohol and the alcohol they excrete kills them off. That is to say they die in their own shit. Or put another way, their eating kills them. Sound familiar? But to make sure, we add sulfites to wipe out every organism still clinging to life."

"Charming, the way you put it."

"Life and death, partner. Hand in hand around the world they go."

Solomon had managed to rent a pump and a bladder press somewhere. As Turghoff crushed the Campden tablets and pushed the powder into the empty barrels, Solomon set up the pump and connected a garden hose to the press. Then while Turghoff was jumping around photographing the various pieces of equipment, Solomon left the room and returned with a bottle of cabernet, two glasses and a jumbo-sized bag of pretzels.

"Don't open that," Turghoff said, raising his hands.

"What? I got this bottle for just this occasion. A small winery in the Sierra foothills. The wine is six years old. It's rich, it's full bodied, you're gonna love it."

"No. I want to drink our wine."

Solomon looked terrified. "No, it's not…"

"I know it's green. I know it hasn't been pressed or filtered. I know it hasn't even touched oak. I know all that. But it is wine. You just said so yourself. And it's our wine. So we pour off a quart. We filter it through a T-shirt and we drink it."

Solomon was shaking his head. "It's not ready. Besides that, we're going to need it all. First, both barrels have to be filled to the brim. If they're not full the wine goes bad. Second, we will need the rest because I will have to top off the barrels now and then as the wine ages."

Turghoff put his hands on his friend's shoulders. "It's going to be all right. We can spare a quart. And it doesn't have to be perfect. This is our first time. We got what we got and I want to try it."

Solomon set the bottle down and sighed. "Okay. But no T-shirt, that's ridiculous. We pass it through the press and then we divert a glass or two before it gets to the barrel. Just a taste."

"A quart."

"Okay, one quart."

Over the rest of the afternoon they pumped the must out of the fermenter and into the press, and the new wine flowed out of the press and into the barrels. They ate every pretzel in the bag and they carefully sipped their wine. It was not bad. It might be even good, they decided, and it promised to get better. Solomon and Turghoff raised their glasses. They looked at each other and laughed.

After they had cleaned everything up, they took showers and went upstairs where Patty and Britt had chicken and wild rice waiting. When Turghoff entered the room wrapped in a borrowed robe, Britt said to him, "Carly Curtiss says you are funny. Say something funny."

Turghoff looked at Britt and then at Patty—she with that mysterious Mona Lisa smile that he never quite captured in the drawing he had done years before—and to the disappointment of everyone, he could not think of a single clever thing to say.

CHAPTER TWENTY-THREE

Turghoff needed his headlights as he drove Old Ugly from the Solomon home to his own. He had stayed too long. He had eaten too much food and drunk too much of Solomon's expensive wine—two bottles carefully chosen to celebrate the day and enhance the chicken. He was tired and he wanted to be in bed. His work was suffering from too much life. That was the insight that came to him. When he got to bed late, he struggled to get up, and when he did get up, he would find himself flat before an empty canvas. Enjoy life too much and the work deteriorated. And the important thing was the work.

It was then that he discovered Yvonne's car parked in the driveway. Rather than turn her away, he made an offer: "I was thinking of twenty minutes in the tub. You interested?"

"I could use that," she said.

They drank water and watched the sky darken and the stars multiply. Neither spoke about their previous time in the spa or the flowers he had sent to *The Woeful*. Maybe Florence had claimed them for herself.

He said: "I telephoned the lawyer in the city. I emailed her the sketch and the letter from the T&I folks and suggested she speak with the tenants if she wanted their thoughts. She promised to run it by the family and get back to me."

"How big is the family?"

"I didn't ask. I don't see why they would object. We'll be adding value to the building. Plus, I told her we'd repaint the entire wall. Not just the stretch where the mural is going. The whole wall from street to alley, from roof to ground. Montoya knows a guy who runs a paint crew. He said the fellow would get his crew to help us."

"I'm sorry, but when I hear the word 'family' I think trouble. In my experience families are unstable and dangerous. And the university?"

She had a way of saying "I'm sorry," when she was not sorry at all.

"I called and spoke with a woman. The department head is at some conference. He's the guy who's supposed to know. I sent the image to her as well. She said he would insist on a personal meeting. Which means I'll have to drive up there one of these days. She'll call me when he's back."

Yvonne sighed. She laid her head against his shoulder and he felt her thigh brush against his.

"He's at AA tonight," she said after a moment, answering the question he had thought but not asked. "And AA makes him intolerable. I didn't marry a preacher but now I got one."

"What's that? An hour or two?"

"It'll be later. He's going more and more native on me. His grandmother on his mother's side was almost full Comanche. And now he's met a couple of native guys at AA. They hang out together drinking coffee and talking about plants, vision quests, purification fasts, things like that. He's into it. He plans to do a sweat one of these weekends. He wants me to go along but sweating is not my thing."

"You're sweating now," Turghoff said, pouring them more water.

Yvonne traced a finger along his thigh. "This is not a sweat, darling. This is an indulgence."

"And Carly?"

Carly, she explained, had been invited to a sleepover. Yvonne did not know the parents, or parent, though she had met the girl once or twice. "I probably should have checked into it. You never know these days, perverts abound. But she wanted to go so badly. She's felt herself on the outside ever since we moved here. She feels like a ghost at school, she told me one time. Like she can see her classmates but they can't see her, or won't see her. Except for Britt, of course. But Britt has many other friends she spends time with."

"Yes."

"So, this was a big deal and she would have hated me if I insisted on calling the mother and embarrassing her. Still, I should have checked. I don't know if she's the only girl staying or if it's a larger group. I don't even know where it is. Gil took her."

"I can't believe he would just pull up to the curb and drop her off."

Yvonne lifted a leg out of the water and let it flop back in. "Well, it's done now."

"And you're here."

"Yes."

"Good," he said. And it was good. He cared about her and he liked being with her. But he was tired and her presence kept him from going to bed. And if he did not get to bed, the work would not go well.

They lazed side by side, and after a while she said: "It's important to distinguish the real from the not real."

"Yes," he said, after a pause. "Yes, it is."

It felt so domestic, the two of them.

He sank deeper into the water. He decided to not include the ball of mistletoe in the painting with the oak branch. It would make for clutter. Just continue with the limb, bare and muscular with its harsh angle. And after the angle, coming off the limb and forward toward the viewer, that smaller branch with its claw-like shoots, the one in the other photo. A hint of menace, that was what he wanted. The claw-like shoots, as if they were reaching out from the canvas. And maybe Carly was right. Maybe along the right edge, a suggestion of the trunk, and that knotty juncture where the branch comes off. He liked the full, muscular look of that joint.

"Meaning, the now from the not now," Yvonne added.

"What?"

"And the here from the not here."

Turghoff yawned. "You mean here and there?"

"No, I mean the here and the not here."

"All right."

The ball of mistletoe, he now realized, deserved a painting of its own. He pictured a square canvas, blue again, and the ball perfectly centered. Yes, it should be relentlessly symmetrical. No branch. Just the mistletoe as if suspended in mid-air. Big, voluptuous but imperfect with a few dead stalks spiraling out. Berries? He would have to think about berries. Berries could get sugary. The challenge would be to make it appear three dimensional. It had to have depth, as if you were seeing into its interior, and the surface should protrude out from the canvas, or seem to.

Turghoff pushed himself out of the water. Not a good idea to be thinking about work just as he was going to bed. He paused, sitting for a moment on the back of the seat.

"I'm going to sleep," he said. "Stay as long as you wish, but I have to work tonight and I need the rest."

Yvonne looked surprised, disappointed.

"I'm sorry, but I do have to go." Then he left for the bedroom, closing the door behind him.

Moments later with the lights out, his body curled, his hands beneath the pillow, he felt ugly, selfish and cruel. When she tiptoed through the darkened room on her way out he feigned sleep.

CHAPTER TWENTY-FOUR

Carly did not mention the sleepover when she came to the studio the following week. She had finally dared to bring some drawings. He found them boring as drawings but managed to hide his disappointment. The magic of her earlier work had been replaced by a careful and rigid exactness. A still life or two, and portraits, mostly of her cat.

He thought of a famous quote taken from Delacroix's journal—something about how a painting, the physical object, was just a pretext, a bridge from the artist's mind to the mind of the viewer. Turghoff found this sentiment obvious on the one hand and meaningless on the other. Wasn't all art—a symphony, a novel, a painting—a bridge from the mind of the composer, novelist, artist to the mind of the listener, reader, viewer? The first question was: How good was the bridge? Could the mind of the viewer be conveyed across this bridge and into the mind of the artist? And more importantly: What was in the mind of the artist? Was the destination worth the journey? Of late he had been seeing bridges constructed with great skill that transported him to minds that seemed to contain little of interest.

But the quality of the bridge was important. For that reason he believed in fundamentals and the formal training required to learn them. Perspective, composition and proportion. The crafting of lines, techniques of shading, the magic of erasers and the need to copy the works of masters, even tracing. But this was not the time for any of that.

He filled Carly with praise. He set her down with marking tools and butcher paper and told her to draw, draw, draw. He left her alone and when he returned he disguised his criticism as tricks. "Try this," he would say.

When he found her working in a small corner of a large sheet of paper, he shouted, "Fill the page! Bigger, bigger, bigger!"

When he saw her worrying over the exact shape of an apple, erasing and scratching and trying to get the curve just right, he commanded her: "Make mistakes, waste paper. Make a thousand mistakes before the sun has set. This will not end up in the Louvre. That's not the point. Let your hand guide you. Free it to move across the page."

When he got her to laugh at herself and at him and then start again, he felt enlivened.

Later, closing the door to the studio and going out to his garden in search of an ear of corn ready for his evening meal, Turghoff asked himself what this thing with Carly was about. Was it just for Yvonne he was doing this? He did enjoy Yvonne's company. They did have fun in the spa and in the bed and his work was going wonderfully most nights. He felt alive, healthy and grateful. In a mood to be generous toward her child.

A fat larva snuggled down at the tip of most every ear, devouring milky kernels at one end while pushing dark waste out the other. This was organic gardening the way it was supposed to be, he thought, bringing the ear to his nose to breathe in the smell of it, his toughened bare feet sunk in the loose garden dirt. He came from the middle west, corn fresh on the cob was built into his genes.

Did he like the kid? Well, he wore shorts now in the afternoons knowing she might stop by. Montoya teased him about it: "Well now, is Turghoff returning to civilization?"

§

Three days later he was in Way Natural picking up some bottled pasta sauce when he saw Ms. Patty Solomon again.

She stood on the other side of the produce section waving the latest edition of *The Woeful* in his direction. She held the paper some distance from her body, suspended at its edge between her thumb and index finger as if she were transporting a poop-filled diaper to the trash.

"I want you to know, Patty, that was not my idea."

Racks of shiny apples and greenish bananas stood between them so he mouthed the words rather than shouting them. But he was close enough to see her eyes roll and her head shake.

"Honest, I had no idea!" he yelled as she turned away with that deprecating smile that was becoming ever more familiar.

It crossed his mind that Patty—who had once set out to circle the globe in a tartan hat, but was now well-settled in her successful familial life—could be experiencing pangs of envy. Of himself and his modest notoriety? Of Yvonne, her risk-taking, unstable friend? The object or the genesis of her annoyance mattered little. Turghoff treasured Patty Solomon as a friend; he felt her displeasure and it troubled him.

It was true that he had had no idea. Yvonne had not spoken about the latest article or run it past him before delivering it to Mel Kline. He, like everyone else, saw it first in the published paper. He had consented to being photographed while standing beside the dented hood of Old Ugly, rumpled and unkempt in his usual shorts and T-shirt. But he could not have imagined that she would place that simple downhome image alongside one that showed him dressed casually artsy and chatting with a glamorous woman six inches taller than himself at a crowded New York opening. The opening, which had occurred several years earlier, had earned him and his work a few generous lines in *The New Yorker*, which, of course, she also quoted.

Yvonne had done her research, he had to credit her that. She had found most every gracious comment and flattering photo that had appeared in some distant urban publication and had worked them into the article. The unmistakable conclusion was that their little town hid a celebrity. The locals were not just getting a mural the article announced; they were getting a Turghoff. The exposure was embarrassing but he was impressed, perhaps for the first time, by how insightful Yvonne was. She had recognized what he had long understood but rarely said aloud, that buyers did not purchase a painting, as a painting. A painting was acquired because it had been created by a particular artist. Buyers wanted to take home and hang on their wall a piece of the person who had created it. As she was always saying: It's you, Turghoff.

She must have been working on the flattering article the last time she came by, but she had not mentioned it. It had been a surprise she was preparing for him, he saw now, something she thought would please him. That was the night he had left her alone in the spa. Her husband was dreaming of vision quests, her daughter was at a sleepover, her lover abandoned her for a good night's sleep. And she had been left alone in the spa, the juicy surprise souring in her gut.

CHAPTER TWENTY-FIVE

Turghoff's unusual hours had required him to design, create and screw onto his front door a notice that read:

READ BEFORE KNOCKING.
The occupant works nights and sleeps mornings.
Do not disturb before noon.
No peddlers, do-gooders or earnest believers at any hour.
I won't buy your product, contribute to your cause, sign your petition, vote for your candidate, or convert to your religion.
Have a nice day.

Handwritten in a large, legible script on a painted slab of plywood, the notice commanded a significant portion of the windowless door. Its bold presence, however, did not prevent someone from pounding continuously on the door at ten on a Tuesday morning a few days following the latest article.

In the dream he was abruptly awakened from, he was walking toward a restaurant to meet someone. A comfortable road became a ruined building that he had to climb over and around. He found himself on a precarious edge; he could no longer turn back, and could proceed only at great risk. When he pulled off his sleep mask, the light was blinding.

At the door stood the beaded, wispy-haired, faux-native woman from the tourist office board. The one said to manage a chain motel at the eastern bypass.

Turghoff was a slow starter. Twenty minutes in the breakfast nook with a cup of coffee were necessary for his normal waking consciousness to assume control. As he fumbled to pull up his shorts, he longed to berate the woman but lacked the coherence necessary. But then she was so busy apologizing, he could not have inserted a sentence had he the ability to do so.

The urgency of the woman's speech astounded him. It was as if they had jumped off a skyscraper and she wanted to tell her life-story before they smashed onto the sidewalk. He caught that her name was Marianne Webster. "You remember? From the meeting?"

He may have nodded.

She belonged to a service club, she told him. "Every week we have a program. Well, not just a program, also lunch and some business items related to our service work. And we fine each other, but don't worry we won't fine you."

Turghoff tried to say he was pleased to hear that, but she had paused only for a quick breath. "The club is meeting today," she stammered. "At noon!" She was responsible for presenting the program, but the scheduled speaker had canceled. "A half hour ago! Can you believe it? The Effects of Drug Use on Prenatal Development, too. How important is that! I was so looking forward to it. But she cancelled."

A sense of dread was seeping into Turghoff's caffeine-free head. Had she said noon? Today?

"Could you come and talk about the murals? Please? I would be so grateful. And you get a free lunch, did I say that? A twenty-minute talk then ten minutes to answer questions. If you've worked up a program on your computer, we could just show that. Then you would only have to answer a few questions. I can't believe that woman cancelled!"

Yvonne had suggested he develop a presentation on his computer to pitch the concept. But he had yet to put it together.

"Anything," Marianne Webster pleaded "I'm in such a bind. Anything at all!"

§

Turghoff was reminded once again how vitality had fled Long Branch when he learned that the meeting was being held in a chain restaurant set beside a service station near the western bypass offramp. When he arrived truckers were refueling, their refrigeration units rumbling, and mothers ran with their children toward restrooms. A decade or more previous, he had attended a meeting of the same service club as a guest. In those days, the meetings were held at The Wagon Wheel, an historic restaurant on Main Street in the heart of downtown with a back room that was large, comfortable and quiet. The restaurant had been closed now for a couple of years, the door boarded up. A couple of young cannabis growers were said to have purchased the building but had done nothing with it.

Turghoff's friend, Terry Clark, had a bookstore located on Cedar just off Main. In one room he had installed a copy machine and a couple of computers you could rent out. He sold books and magazines and most anything else that might help pay the rent, including knickknacks for kids and greeting cards, some of which featured Turghoff's artwork. Terry carried his lunch from the service line and set it down across from Turghoff.

"Are you in this club?" Turghoff asked, surprised.

Terry shook his head to indicate the affirmative and at the same time bafflement. "They're desperate," he muttered, looking around. "Well, that's not fair. The good old boys are trying to bridge the gap. Gotta give them credit for the effort. The timber wars are over, pot's sort of legal now, and my hair has at last become iconic." Terry stroked his gray ponytail. "The reasons they had to hate us are mostly gone, so they invited a few of us in. Women too, can you believe it? Made the humor cleaner, to bring in the ladies. So, according to last week's bulletin you are here to talk about the effects of drug use on prenatal development. The breadth of your knowledge never ceases to impress me, Turghoff." Terry's eyes were twinkling.

"She canceled I was told. You're looking at the poor substitute."

"The murals."

"That's right."

"Good. By the way, you've got yourself quite a promoter in that reporter. The woman's got an edge about her, and she can write."

"You know her?"

Terry shrugged. "She's been in the store a couple of times with her kid. I know her husband better. Nice guy."

"So, you know..." Turghoff brightened; this was the first promising thing that had happened since the sun came up.

"Curtiss. Yeah, Gil Curtiss. He's a vet."

Turghoff nodded. Another war, another time, but still a vet. Terry had been drafted and sent to Nam as an eighteen-year-old. He came back an anti-war radical, but he had never lost his solidarity with other veterans.

"I haven't met him," Turghoff said. He was working through a generous slab of lasagna, and eying the square of brown cake with its little swirl of whipped cream. He shouldn't, but he knew he would.

"Drives a propane truck, likes to fish." Terry paused before adding: "He saw some stuff over there. It doesn't matter if you're in a jungle or walking on sand, the shit's the same. And it's slow to fade."

Turghoff nodded. He touched his fork to the whipped cream. He wanted to know more but he did not want to appear to want to know more.

Terry clearly had no qualms about the lasagna. He took a large bite.

"You know the kind of guy," he said, chewing. "You probably met him in high school. Sort of smart, sort of funny, but kind of shy. Sort of fat but not too fat; he hangs at the edge of the crowd but not out of it. He's the guy who if you stopped to listen to him, if you took the time to really know him, you would be impressed. Well, anyway, Gil's that guy. In this violent, capitalist culture, it's like Odysseus and the sirens getting past the recruiters. Gil's smart, but he's not Odysseus and the sirens snared him. But he is smart enough and decent enough that the shit that happens in war had the power to really damage him."

Turghoff nodded, tasting the cake. "I believe in this project, Terry. The murals will be good for me, good for you, good for the town."

"Then get up there and sell it." Terry motioned with a finger. "But first, swipe that whipped cream off your mustache."

CHAPTER TWENTY-SIX

Yvonne Curtiss was not happy: "Last week I made you a hero. This week you ignore me." She was on the phone an hour after the meeting. "Will you be there? I'm coming over."

Her problem was that Turghoff had not told her he was presenting the program. Had she known, she would have wangled an invitation from her editor. He was a member of the club and she could have gotten a story out of it.

"I didn't know I was presenting the program until this morning," he protested. "That Webster woman woke me out of a sound sleep and nearly dragged me there."

"You could have called. Fifteen seconds on the phone and I would have been there. As it is, he's writing the story."

"She wanted a bio. I had to get the artwork together, I had to find my notes. I hadn't even had my coffee when she came banging on the door."

Yvonne was not impressed. At his house a few minutes later, she paced back and forth in the kitchen, her arms folded across her chest as if she were protecting her heart from his unfair behavior.

"I don't receive a salary, Turghoff, just so you know. I get paid by the column inch, okay. No story, no money."

"I didn't know," Turghoff said, somewhat surprised.

"Not only that, Kline doesn't want to do the story. He thinks it's my fault I didn't know you were doing the program. Kline is a lazy son of a bitch who'd rather spend his time putting together ad copy or searching the Internet for porn or penny loafers or whatever it is he searches for.

"Because the whole operation is run on a shoestring, and because he was there, and because he usually writes some dribble about the weekly club program, he feels obligated to write the story. And, in case you haven't noticed, Kline is a lousy writer. Trust me, he will do you no favors. The man's a master of the mixed metaphor, the confused simile, the blandly obvious parading without irony. So, what he does write about the mural project will likely put everyone but his mother to sleep. Fortunately for him, if not for us, his mother owns the paper."

Turghoff knew Mel Kline. He knew Mel's mother, Florence, by sight. Mel's father, the late Mike Kline, ran the paper back when Turghoff and Alicia first arrived. The Klines were considered the town's intellectual family back then. Mike put out a lively weekly paper, Florence taught piano and young Mel was said to be a prodigy at the keyboard.

Turghoff explained this to Yvonne and then said, "Mike Kline was known for hard work and hard drink. One stormy night he drove off the old bridge—the west bridge that took you across the river before the bypass was put in. His car landed nose down on the river bank thirty feet below. Mike somehow managed to get out; he climbed up to the road and made it home where Florence hid him until he sobered up. It happened before I got here, but it was a famous story back then. I remember the bridge but it was dismantled shortly after we arrived. Mel and his mother still live in the same house, that old two-story next to the Catholic church."

"The Incestuary," Yvonne said, scowling.

"Some call it that, but there's no evidence they're anything but mother and half-grown son."

"They bicker like an old married couple, I can tell you that. And that story about the father, that's the kind of sick romance that builds up around drunks: drunks as tough guys, drunks as heroes. Stories like that piss me off. Florence should have called the cops when the old man crawled into the house and had him hauled off to meet his fate."

Yvonne grabbed her purse off the counter and pulled out the bottle of pills. For a moment she held it cupped in her hand as if it were a talisman. Then she slowly slid it back into the purse. The act moved Turghoff in a way he found surprising.

She was in a war with that stuff, he realized. He had not recognized that before.

"I live in two worlds," she said, not looking at him. "They exist simultaneously and I go back and forth between them. One is the everyday: mothering Carly, monitoring Gil, putting food on the table, getting some sleep, paying the bills. The other is pain. Pain is featureless other than levels of intensity. But it's always there. I am always in it or at the edge of it."

Her admission stunned him. He had enjoyed a fortunate life to date; he had avoided broken bones, major surgeries and the dreaded C. He had felt pain of course: toothaches, headaches, a fingernail ripped loose a few years ago, blows to the testicles as a kid, a badly sprained ankle when he was nineteen, the Headlong-induced spasms that sent him crawling to Solomon's office. He had known pain. But for him pain was transitory. It existed as a sensation he went into and came out of. She seemed to be describing pain as a permanent feature of her psyche, a presence that rose and receded but never disappeared. It was as if she were trapped in a cage and pain was a roaring lion she needed to keep at bay, if not with a whip and a chair, then a pill.

So foreign to him was this concept that he doubted her. Pain was not like that. Pain followed injury. Pain was a byproduct, a part of the healing process. Okay, she had suffered injuries, fractures to the leg, something with the neck. Obviously there would have been a lot of pain. But the accident had happened more than a year ago. The bones would have healed and the pain should be gone by now. Pain did not possess an independent existence like a poinsettia in a planter or a moon of Saturn.

Back when they first moved to town, he and Alicia had known the Klines quite well. Later Jen had studied piano with Florence. Mel gave recitals at the Lutheran church and Jen turned pages for him. What Turghoff remembered now, was how some crisis would always happen to Mel just before a performance. A flicker of lights and the power would go off moments before he was to go on stage; the piano would suddenly go out of tune, and the tuner called in desperation; one time a yellowjacket flew into the sanctuary where Mel was doing a last run-through and stung him on the tip of his finger. In the end, the recital always happened but it seemed to require a crisis to precede it. Is that what Yvonne was doing? Was she inventing some obstacle in her life that she would then have to climb over?

And what effect would her drama have on the mural project? Or on his life?

"Where am I in this?" Turghoff felt compelled to ask.

"I thought you were neither. You took me out of both. That was the good thing about us. But today you complicated the first and increased the level of the second." She picked up her purse and slung the strap across her shoulder.

Turghoff may have frowned.

"I don't know if Mel told you, but the club offered me a thousand dollars for the project. Good news, eh? A grand, but I couldn't take it."

"No, he did not tell me. But, of course you should not take it. It's not your money, not really."

"Exactly. So, what should I do? Terry Clark said something about setting up a non-profit."

"No, no, that'll take months. We need to find an existing one. We go back to the Tourist and Information folks and we have them open a bank account dedicated to the mural. The club writes a check to T&I and we deposit it there."

Turghoff was not convinced. "I don't want to *own* the money but I *do* want to control it. If they get their fingers on it, who knows what will happen."

Yvonne nodded. "You're right. They'll get crummy about it. A group mind is a frightening beast, both scared and scary. My time as a military wife convinced me of that." She paused, staring at a corner of the ceiling. "So, we need to control the money, and they need assurances that the funds won't be misused, thus tarnishing their precious reputations. That's the idea, right?"

She seemed suddenly buoyant, as if just holding the bottle of pills had altered her chemistry.

He nodded, accepting her description, though he was not comfortable about the "we" part. Was this not his project and was she not just a reporter writing about it?

"Tell you what I'll do," Yvonne announced. "I will go to the credit union, talk to them about an account. Then I'll stop by the T&I office, and have a chat with the manager, you know, the chunky gal, Joanie, I think it is, the one taking notes at the meeting. I'll figure it out, and who knows, maybe I'll wangle a story out of it."

Then turning toward the door, she said, "That woman you got who comes here to clean?"

"Yeah, Lisa, Montoya's friend."

"She's short, right?"

"Yeah, why?"

Yvonne pointed out some cobwebs in the ceiling's corners. Some of them were black with age. They had probably been there since Jen left and Turghoff had never noticed them.

"Anyway, gotta go. Maybe I can make a buck before the sun goes down. We left a mountain of debt back in Santa Rosa."

CHAPTER TWENTY-SEVEN

The next time Carly came over, Turghoff got down his coffee-table book of Ansel Adams photographs. "One time, you asked why my snapshots of tree branches on the hillside are not art. Well, this book contains art created by a photographer. And today, we're going to experience the difference."

They sat on the couch and he placed the book in her lap and told her to not open it. Then he spread his photographs out on the coffee table in front of them.

"First, I want us to look again at my photographs, and then we'll study six of Ansel's photographs. Just six today, slowly without rushing. It doesn't matter which six. Every image in this book is a treasure. Then, after the six, we will take a second look at my photos. That's the game, okay? I'm not going to say anything, and I don't want you to speak either. We just look and absorb."

"Why just six?"

"Good question, but we will save that for later. So, first my snapshots."

He lifted them one by one, looked at each and handed it to her. When they had finished, he opened the Adams book at random and placed it on the table: two images appeared, one on each page. Several minutes later, he turned the page and carefully flattened the book. Each of the Adams photographs was familiar to Turghoff, each a friend of long acquaintance. Still, so intense was the experiment for him that he forgot at times that Carly was sitting beside him. Had she been bored? Was she fidgeting, looking around for Jocko? He did not remember.

He wanted to point out the differences, the similarities. He wanted to make comparisons, talk about composition, about light, about focus, cropping, about tension. But he restrained himself. Just let her look, he kept telling himself. Let her explore her own path.

After he had closed the book and as he was directing her attention back to the snapshots, he sensed a darkening in the room. Turning, he saw a large man standing in the doorway.

§

Turghoff experienced a sense of completion at that moment, a feeling of, Oh yes, of course. It was if he had just watched a cue ball strike the eight ball which brushed the edge of the seven ball which then rolled slowly toward a hole and dropped in. Inevitable, obvious… once it had happened.

"Dad!" Carly jumped up. The photographs falling from her hands onto the floor.

Yes, large, Turghoff thought, himself struggling to gain his footing. He saw a bulky man in the doorway, fleshy but not obese. No glasses, dark hair but none on the face. A blue work uniform, a necklace caught in the hairs below his throat.

"Come in," Turghoff stammered, distracted by the book in his hand, the useless damn photos on the floor.

Carly had run to the doorway and thrown her arms around her father's waist.

"You must be…" Turghoff stumbled toward the two of them.

"Curtiss," the man said, nodding. His voice soft, not apologetic exactly, but not a declaration either.

"Carly's…" Turghoff started.

"Yes, Yvonne's…" The man remained in the doorway.

"Of course."

Their hands met and shook and there followed an uncomfortable pause.

The man was curious, it seemed to Turghoff, his eyes flitting around taking in the room.

"Would you..?" Turghoff began.

"Your things?" Gil Curtiss said, looking down at his daughter.

"…like to come in for a minute?"

"Ahh…"

"A glass of…" Good God, what was he thinking. He could not offer the man a beer or a glass of wine. "No… a cup of tea perhaps?"

"You have to meet Jocko, Dad."

Gil Curtiss hesitated, then nodded slightly and stepped inside.

"Pick up those pictures," he half-whispered to his daughter as they approached the couch.

§

Turghoff's second wife had been a tea person. Jen believed in ceremony. When people came through the door she always offered them tea and then busied herself putting on the pot and organizing the service as she talked. That memory struck him now as he stepped into the kitchen; the image of her moving about. She had maintained a store of cookies, biscuits, but those were long gone.

"Take a seat anywhere, and don't worry about the photos." This over his shoulder.

He had no love for tea. It burned his tongue and cooled too quickly and it always seemed to irritate his throat. Beyond making crunchy things mushy, it served no purpose in his experience other than increasing his urge to urinate. But in the cupboard he did locate a cluttering of small bright boxes. They felt almost weightless and their "best if used before" dates had long passed, though when brought to his nose whiffs of aroma rose to greet him.

"Herbal okay?" he shouted as he filled the pot and brought a flame to life on the stove.

Moments later Turghoff cautiously entered the living room balancing a tray with Jen's second-best (she had taken the first) hand-painted ceramic pot snug in its cozy, three cups, spoons, a handful of stale saltines and a few dried chunks of bread. The Curtiss father and daughter were on the couch leafing through the Ansel Adams book. On Carly's lap Jocko looked smugly superior.

"So," he said, setting the tray on the coffee table and himself in a chair. "This has to steep." Then, after a long pause, the three of them staring at the pot, "I knew a guy worked at NewFuel for years. Damion... something Irish, O'Leary. Yes, O'Leary. Ten or so years older than me. Volunteered with the fire department as well. I put in a stint there myself years ago, the fire department, that is. Willie Gardner was captain back then."

"His wife died," Gil Curtiss said.

"Willie's?"

"No, Damion's. Willie I don't know."

"Damion's, I'm sorry to hear that."

"Cancer."

"That's tough. My wife knew her. Jen, my former wife. They grew chickens."

Gil looked surprised. "Your wife and Damion's wife grew chickens?"

"No, sorry. Damion and his wife grew chickens, and my wife got eggs from her. What was her name? Bel? Bella?"

"Yes, Bella."

"She worked at the school-district office back then. In the spring, when the chickens were really laying, Jen would stop by the office and buy a dozen from her. Very fresh, very good eggs. The yolks were yellow as the sun and they held together round as globes when you plopped them in the grease."

"He retired not long after I came on."

"Damion."

"Yeah, after his wife died. Then he moved somewhere. Idaho, I think."

"Good guy, Damion. Sorry to hear about Bella."

"Yeah, seemed like it."

Carly was trying to interest Jocko in a piece of bread. Looking up she said, "Do you think it's ready?"

The two men looked at her confused.

"The tea?" She pointed.

"Ahh." Turghoff picked up the warm pot and filled the three cups, the mint flavor rising with the steam. He realized that he had forgotten to place milk and sugar on the tray, a mistake Jen would never have made. He asked, but both declined, so they drank their tea straight.

The object at the base of Curtiss's throat caught his attention. A strip of rawhide circled his neck and hanging from it was a stone arrowhead bound by copper wire. The necklace reminded him of his first wife. Alicia had been a jeweler. She used to polish silver and semi-precious stones and wrap them in wire to fashion earrings, necklaces and such.

Gil Curtiss was saying, "Lots of windows."

"Yeah, I like light." Turghoff responded absently as his attention returned to the present. But then after an uncomfortable pause during which he watched Curtiss actively scrutinize every wall and corner of the room, he added: "It's a funny thing about light. Most artists want to work in natural light…I love light as much as the next guy, but I do most of my painting at night. So, artificial light. Some people claim you cannot create true color in artificial light, but I have not found that to be a problem."

"And no shades," Gil Curtiss added

Robert Turghoff looked around. "No. Well, the house is set back from the road." He felt defensive, as if he had to justify his house, or at least its security. "I don't feel exposed."

"So, look, Dad." Carly took up a photograph from the table and showed it to her father. "Okay, now look at this." She opened the book and pointed toward the page. "He says the photos in this book are art, and the one I'm holding is not art. And he wants me to figure out why. So, what do you think?"

"That's nice," Gil Curtiss said. He carefully placed his cup on the tray and brushed the few breadcrumbs off his lap. "We need to get going. Grandma and Grandpa called to say they are driving up. They're taking us to dinner."

§

After they left, Robert Turghoff sat for a long time in the chair facing the couch, his cup of tea cooling beside him. A layer of clouds came up the river dimming the afternoon light. And with the clouds a bit of wind, and the wind caused the small leaves of the plum tree outside his near window to swirl about as if agitated. Summer was departing, he realized, and autumn had arrived.

Several years earlier he had done a series of paintings, some large, some small, he called The Year of the Plum. The series began with the tree winter-bare, then a branch where the first nodules brought the promise of white flowers. Next came a portrait of the tree filled with flowers, then a twig with the first tender leaves appearing amid wilting petals. Another showed the trunk rising from a carpet white with fallen petals. Filling one canvas was the tree in its splendor, thickly green with new leaves. A long narrow piece portrayed a branch strung with the first hints of shiny green fruit. A second presented the same branch, its abundant fruit turning purple. This was followed by the earth stained with purple fruit. Another presented the leaves gone yellow and pale-green just as the tree looked now outside his window. The final canvas—and the largest in the series—showed the tree with its branches bare, the trunk rising through a blanket of decomposing brown and black leaves. That had been his favorite image: those sodden decaying leaves shading from light brown to black had suggested to him an animal's pelt patterned so that when looked upon, the creature would not be seen.

He had been excited about the project and had devoted several months to its completion. The plum's year spoke to him of all life, its birth and potential, its glories and inevitable decline. But only a few of the paintings sold. Several still hung forgotten on the shadowy back wall of a distant gallery; others were stacked away in his studio.

This August and September he had eaten plums off the ground as they fell and he had plucked a few from the lower branches. He offered a bag to Yvonne but after a taste she found the skin thick and annoying and refused to take them. The plums were gone now and some of the leaves had begun to yellow and the gusting wind sent them fluttering onto the driveway where they formed a dense yellow and green carpet.

His mind could not hold the beautiful image of falling leaves. It wanted to review the strange encounter that had just happened. Polite, civil but awkward, hesitant; Gil Curtiss making sly glances about the room, fondling his teacup. Was he imagining his daughter in this room? And how surprising that Carly as she left, honoring her father's instruction to thank Mr. Turghoff, had rushed back and kissed him on the cheek. Never before that moment, had she touched him, or he her.

Or could Curtiss have been imagining his wife in this room? Does he suspect, even know? Might she not have told him? Announced it in a fit of rage? At the heart of an intimate relationship where love and pain boil and mix, vulnerabilities can generate cruelties beyond imagining. Do they fight, he had asked Carly. All the time, she had responded.

Turghoff could not delete the image of the man sitting in a bathtub a pistol in his hand. A gun owner, twisted and tormented by war. He who was ready to point a gun at himself could quickly point it toward another. Could he have been calculating a point of entry as he looked about?

That was absurd, Turghoff told himself; his mind was on a rant. What he should have done was take Curtiss out to the studio. That was his true home where he lived his best hours, and where he and Carly normally spent their time together. But out there, leaning against one wall was his portrait of the man's wife, alluring, mysterious, powerful.

CHAPTER TWENTY-EIGHT

The next time Robert Turghoff saw Gil Curtiss was at the Arts and Crafts Festival, an annual event set on a long green next to the river behind the Branscomb Inn. The event stretched from a mainstage at one end to a smaller stage at the other. Rock bands amped away at one end, while earnest folk singers plucked acoustic guitars at the other. Between the stages two rows of stands featured potters, leather crafters, political advocates, tie-dyers, vintners, face painters, coffee roasters, belly-dancers and a woman who sold tamales that felt warm and comforting in the hand.

Turghoff arrived with Montoya and his son Edgar who was grousing that the festival did not more closely resemble a midway. Headlong wanted to take potshots at a target or at least throw a few baseballs at a stack of bottles. "Bunch of tofu eaters," he announced, a comment that brought an approving chuckle from his plumber father.

Headlong wore a white shirt, black slacks and carried a violin case. The shirt collar was buttoned tightly against his thick throat. With his dark hair parted and matted down he resembled an early-teen wannabe dictator. Except for the violin case. He and his fellow Suzuki violin students were performing on the minor stage in less than an hour. He was said to be a phenomenon as a young fiddler. Montoya or, more often, the boy's mother, drove him to contests hours away where he won ribbons and trophies. "He does classical too," Montoya said. Edgar nodded, "Yeah, I'm already in Book Four."

At a booth selling locally made jewelry Edgar and Carly Curtiss greeted one another. "Hi," one of them said. "Hi," the other responded. Each did a little twitch of a dance to make clear that this was just a casual encounter and they were both cool and unashamed of being in such close proximity.

"You playing?"

"Yeah."

"Cool."

Headlong shrugged. "Just a group thing. The whole class doing 'Twinkle' and stuff."

"Still…"

"Yeah."

They twitched.

Turghoff noticed the back of a woman in a white sleeveless blouse examining the jewelry display. The pale arms and shoulders marked here and there with imperfections were unac-customed to the sun; their appearance suggested an uncomfort-able accommodation to warmth and the out-of-doors. Then he realized that the arms and shoulders belonged to Yvonne. He was surprised to see her in white and then to feel toxic jolts of desire and repulsion race through him. Repulsion not at her but at the desire filling him.

Gil Curtiss stood beside her, caught in a web. That was the way it struck Turghoff. As if the man were held in place by strands of invisible fiber; a man beside his wife but not with her, standing next to his daughter but separated from her, his gaze focused on the distant redwoods across the river.

"Hey," Turghoff said when Gil Curtiss turned toward them.

"Hey." Curtiss nodded.

"You know Montoya?

Gil Curtiss shook his head, and Turghoff introduced them.

"Annual thing," he explained. "This festival was hap-pening years before I got here. Decades. It was a big deal at first they tell me. Hippies popping up like wildflowers in logger land, a kind of cultural invasion. Instead of some guy in a hardhat using a chainsaw to carve a bear from a log, you had a gal in a tie-dye blouse and a full skirt reading Tarot cards."

Montoya said: "When I first came here, every year sometime in August, a dozen people held a demonstration at the intersection of Main and Redwood protesting the bombing of Hiroshima. I mean that was like what, forty years earlier the bomb exploded? They were protesting a thing that had happened before they were even born. As they drove by, the hippies honked and cheered while the rednecks booed and gave the finger. That's the way it was back then."

Cultural history seemed to bore Gil Curtiss. He returned his gaze to the tall trees across the river. "Is that the campground over there?"

"Yeah," Montoya said. "That's state park land but you access the campground from the other end. Must be fifty, a hundred sites in those trees."

Curtiss nodded. "I walked through there a few weeks ago. Height of the camping season and it was almost empty. I was surprised to find so few tents."

Turghoff thought about that. "That is interesting. I guess people don't camp like they used to."

"But they do," Curtiss insisted. "Just walk along the river, or hike in that patch of brush at the base of Big Hill."

Montoya laughed. "Yeah, well, but those aren't campers, man. Those are homeless guys living in…"

"Camps," Curtiss said, completing Montoya's sentence.

"Right," Montoya admitted. "Just no toilet facilities, no charge, no law, no trash pickup. Definitely no trash pickup."

"And within walking distance of downtown," Turghoff said. "That state campground is two or more miles from downtown. You need to be closer in if you're going to panhandle and get yourself some food and booze."

"That's right," Montoya said.

"They're my brothers in arms," Curtiss said quietly. "Walking casualties of our several wars, at least some of them."

Turghoff and Montoya looked at one another.

"Are they beyond repair?" Turghoff asked.

Gil Curtiss looked at him closely and it seemed to Turghoff it was the first time the two of them had made real eye contact.

"You can't fix them, if that's what you mean by repair," Curtiss said to him. "But they are not beyond self-repair, if they choose."

"Okay."

"We choose and we live with the consequences."

"Yes."

"And refusing to choose is just another choice."

In the silence that followed, Turghoff thought of Sergei, his body-building sculptor friend, and Alicia, his first wife. In their student days she and Sergei used to argue about existentialism and free will until Turghoff's eyes glazed over. Then one day Sergei hopped into his Corvette and drove to his death, and a few months later he and Alicia got married and moved west.

Meanwhile Edgar was devising plans of his own. He pushed the violin case into Turghoff's arms and began peeling the buttons free on his white shirt and kicking off his sneakers.

"Me, I want to swim."

"You're on in twenty minutes, man." Montoya sounded desperate as he caught the shirt and then the pants.

"At least he had the swimsuit underneath," Turghoff observed as they watched the lad race toward the river.

Carly Curtiss stood pointing. "He's…?"

"His mother will kill me. She will absolutely kill me. I had him dressed. His hair was combed. We remembered the violin. I got him here on time…" Montoya was holding the white shirt at arm's length as if trying to conjure his son's body back into it.

"Can I go in?" Carly wanted to know.

"Absolutely not," her mother said, grabbing the girl's shoulder. She stared now at Turghoff and then her husband. "Have you two…?"

"Why not? He went!"

"Yes," Turghoff said. They watched Montoya run toward the river waving his son's shirt, pants and sneakers in the air.

CHAPTER TWENTY-NINE

Late morning a few days later, Robert Turghoff sat at his table wearing sweats and having his coffee and breakfast eggs. Yvonne Curtiss sat across from him talking.

She had snuck in through the back door, stripped and climbed into his bed. He had found her there grinning at him when he woke. She liked being in charge, the comings and goings up to her, what they did and what they did not do. He had no problem with that. The stealth, the element of surprise seemed to energize her spirit, and her spirit energized him and his work in the studio. In his mind, the connection was inexplicable and nonlinear but obvious.

She was talking about a new way to promote the mural, and, as Turghoff realized, a way to get paid for yet another article. With his drawing of the proposed mural she had walked around town, showed the image to people and gotten their reactions.

"You and I, we think everybody already knows about this. We're in the middle of it, so we assume everyone is. But that's not true. A few locals I interviewed had never heard of the project. 'Mural?' one said, 'What mural?' Others had only a vague idea."

Her draft of the article lay between them. He felt grateful that she had had the courtesy, this time, to show it to him before passing it on to Mel Kline. But when he reached for the papers, she slapped his hand and grabbed them up. It was her article, damn it, and she was going to read it to him herself. A creator's love for her creation, a feeling he understood perfectly. She insisted on giving her words their best possible reading, just as he would want his painting hung on the best wall of the gallery at the right height, in the light most favorable.

The piece was clever, funny. She had interspersed the citizens' comments about the mural with her own observations about the town, the people she interviewed and, of course, the artist himself. He felt cringey about the neverending self-promotion, or the secondhand self-promotion. A reporter was not a press agent, as Patty Solomon had pointed out weeks ago. But she had become a press agent, and more. In the subtext of the article, it seemed to him, though he did not express this to her, she was hinting at their affair. Was he hearing that right? And if so why?

Turghoff found the energy swirling around him and Yvonne baffling and complex, ambiguous and multidirectional. Wherever he went these days people made mention of the mural and the articles promoting it. The high school art teacher hailed him outside the post office one afternoon and urged him to visit his classes. "The students want to learn more about the project. Can they be involved? And perhaps we could invite that journalist as well. She's one hell of a writer, that gal." (When he mentioned this to Yvonne, she said: "Well, they're accustomed to reading Mel Kline. What can you expect?")

Then the next day, a member of the Civics Club, a gathering of senior ladies, called to invite him to a meeting and "of course bring that young woman writer with you. We would love to hear her story at the same time."

Now, as she bit into a piece of his toast, Yvonne repeated her message: "It's you, Turghoff. The project is you. If you succeed, the mural appears on the wall; if you fail, it fails."

Yes, he thought, it was about me and it was about the mural, but it was also about Yvonne Curtiss. The elevator was going up and both of them were rising with it. Did that bother him? Was he, like Patty Solomon, experiencing a hint of jealousy as Yvonne's reputation climbed and threatened to pass his own? He felt good at this moment with her sitting across from him, and he could not detect in himself any sign that he resented her mounting fame in the community. No, he felt excited for her, pleased to be part of it.

He was not jealous, but he was, he realized, somewhat uncomfortable. He had previously discounted Patty's alarmist talk about his involvement with Yvonne being a threat to her or to her marriage because Yvonne was an adult, and she had been and remained a consenting, even eager participant in their affair. But now as he watched her happily devouring what remained of his toast, he saw something innocent and childlike about her. If her marriage was truly fragile and she truly vulnerable as Patty claimed, did those conditions not weaken the validity of her consent and increase his responsibility? That idea entered his mind for the first time and he did not enjoy finding it there.

A few moments later he learned that her visit was also a pretext for something other than the article or the sex. She wanted to talk about her husband. How had Turghoff met Gil? Had he initiated the contact? Had he lured her husband in some way? She sounded almost jealous.

Turghoff's defense was feeble, and his voice sounded whiny, even to him. "He showed up. I didn't invite him. What can I tell you? He came by to pick up Carly. Something about your parents taking you out to dinner. I like him though. He seems like a decent guy."

Busy digging into her black purse, Yvonne appeared not to be listening.

"Does he know?" Turghoff asked, desperation entering his voice. "That's what I couldn't figure out. Does he know about us?"

Yvonne pulled an object from her purse; she slid it free from a handkerchief and slapped it on the table.

"Howard Piggott's junk shop," she announced triumphantly. "Piggott. You know, the guy with the souped-up wheelchair. That dude is a danger to every able-bodied man, woman and child. But you can find anything you want in that place. He even had a leather strop, can you believe it? I picked them both up for five bucks."

For an instant Turghoff failed to identify what lay before him though he recognized the beauty of its sleek, eye-pleasing curve. Then it struck him. He took the object in hand and pulling the gleaming blade free, brushed his finger along the edge. Very sharp, he thought. Yes, sharp as a razor.

He looked at her. He started to speak and then stopped.

"I collect things," she said, casually flipping her left wrist, a gesture that caused the line of silver bracelets to rattle like chirping birds. She reclaimed the razor, closed it and again wrapped it in the slate-gray handkerchief.

Turghoff felt flummoxed. What did the razor have to do with anything? Was there some text or subtext that he was failing to understand? After a pause and having nowhere else to go, he returned to his previous question:

"So, does he know…about us?"

She shrugged. "Probably. He's very intuitive."

"But…"

She slid the wrapped razor back into her purse. "What goes on between my husband and me, Turghoff, is personal, private and none of your business."

"Of course, but…"

"Don't mess with us, that's what I'm saying. Don't hurt him in any way. And the same goes for Carly. I appreciate the time you spend with her. She talks about you a lot. Really, I'm happy that she's having the experience. But you are a man, Turghoff, and she is a girl, soon to be a young woman, and that scares the hell out of me."

Yvonne stood up. She grabbed the draft article, folded the sheets of paper and pushed them into her mysterious purse.

"So, great to see you. I'm off to meet with good old Mel. Mr. Cliché himself. Did you read the article he did last week about the new crop of high school cheerleaders? That was a piece of work. Take a good look. Mark every time he uses the words 'innocent' or 'sweet' or 'charming' and replace them with 'voluptuous' or 'hot' and you'll get some idea of what the man was actually thinking. Anyway, thanks for the coffee."

CHAPTER THIRTY

A man sat on the sidewalk, leaning against the front door of a defunct clothing store. His feet were bare, his tangled hair hung around his neck and bearded face. Beside him was a thin, dun-colored dog with a rat-like tail and a hunched back that suggested it had been injured in some way. One end of a length of twine had been tied around the puppy's neck, the other was tethered to the man's right ankle. Before them stood a Styrofoam cup looking to be filled with cash. A sign in the man's hand read: "Mama said to wait here."

Rare Apparel, the store in question, had been owned and managed by Sonja Clark, a woman in her late twenties and the daughter of Terry Clark and his first wife, whose name Turghoff could never remember. The store had featured sporty items for younger women: slacks, racy tops, jaunty hats, boots and sandals. Turghoff used to buy small items from Sonja and send them to his daughter Marta. But Sonja had closed it down following the Christmas season at the end of last year. According to Terry, she was hardly making rent. She left a short time later for Seattle hoping to start a new life, and was now working as a barista.

Turghoff had enjoyed Sonja's window displays. She had composed them artfully featuring diagonal lines, contrasting shapes and vivid colors. But viewed now through the empty windows, the vacant interior had the gloomy, shadow-filled look of a discarded dream.

A sheet of plywood had been slapped against the front door and its surface scrawled with garish, unintelligible graffiti in red and black. The man sat with his back against the door and as Turghoff approached he was surprised to realize that the dark figure crouching on the man's far side was Yvonne Curtiss, notebook in hand.

"Originally from Albany," she told Turghoff a few minutes later.

They had slipped into the Long Branch Café two doors down Main Street from the shuttered clothing store. Having predated the construction of the bypass, the Café was a venerable breakfast and lunch diner, famous for its neon sign which blinked on and off revealing a chef flipping his pancake over and over. It had been ten days since he last saw her.

"He heard there was money to be made out here trimming weed. But it wasn't true."

They took seats across from each other in a maroon, Naugahyde booth and Tanya, the waitress, delivered cups of coffee. The coffee was the old-fashioned kind, percolated in a pot and poured into handled, ceramic cups. Not a great coffee but the refills were endless. Perched along counter stools and facing the mirror opposite were three of the town's good old boys. He could hear their murmuring voices and occasional chuckles as they rolled dice and recycled stale gossip.

"Would you hire him?" Turghoff asked Yvonne. "To trim weed or to do anything else?"

"No, but the sign is clever. Let's give him credit for that."

Turghoff agreed. "It is clever and I did give him credit. I gave him a quarter's worth of credit. We share something, he and I. I paint pictures and he makes a little joke. Neither has any intrinsic value but if the world reacts favorably we both receive a bit of money."

Yvonne grinned but it seemed to Turghoff that he saw as much wince as grin in her expression.

"Looked at in that way, buddy, your quarter was rather chintzy."

"Yes, chintzy is the word. And you? Are you doing all right?"

"It was the crouch," she admitted. "Not a good idea for me to crouch on the sidewalk. I was trying to interview him. I want to do an article on the local homeless population. Lift them off the curb and give them names and histories. That's the idea. Mel is adamantly opposed but Florence encouraged me.

'Last thing we need to do is humanize them,' Mel said. Wish I could work that into the piece, but not even Florence could save me if I quoted her son saying that." She paused. "Though I'm not sure Mel would catch the irony if I did."

Turghoff sipped his coffee. He had no desire to insert himself into a triangle composed of Yvonne Curtiss, Mel and Florence Kline. As he watched, Yvonne cautiously stretched her back.

"Do you have a doctor around here, Turghoff? Somebody you could recommend? Mine's getting cranky."

Turghoff looked at her. He had never gotten that razor completely out of his mind and he wanted to ask about it. She collects things. So what does she collect?

But she was clearly uncomfortable and may be in pain, and he said to himself: *I feel bad that she is in pain but there is nothing I can do to help her. Say nothing, do nothing. You may love her but you cannot help her. You will only get sucked into her problems. You are an artist not a counselor. Drink the coffee, pick up the fucking tab and walk out the door.*

Tanya stopped at their booth and topped up their cups.

"So, how's Vince?" she asked Turghoff, setting the pot on the table. "He doesn't do social media I guess."

"No, not Vince. He writes letters. I get one now and then. I could give you his address. He would probably enjoy hearing from you."

Tanya looked puzzled. "You mean like with a pen and a piece of paper?"

Turghoff nodded. "Yeah, that kind. Envelopes, stamps. That is his preferred means of communication. You might find it interesting. You send a letter off and then a few days or weeks later you might get one back."

"That is totally awesome!" Tanya picked up the coffee pot and hurried away.

Yvonne and Turghoff looked at each other.

"I met the head of the Native Studies department at the university," he told her. "Yesterday. I showed him the proposed mural. He didn't see anything wrong with the clothing the native guy is wearing."

"That's good." Yvonne said, grimacing again as she tilted her head to the side.

"Not really. The guy said the mural itself was fraudulent. I think that's the word he used. That it demonstrated a clearly European bias."

"Bias? One native, one white? Both the same gender? How is that bias?"

"That's what I asked and he was happy to tell me. 'You people' he said. Yes, he actually used the words 'you people.' 'You people are so conditioned to individuality that you can't imagine a group sensibility.' The essence of aboriginal life, he said, was group sensibility and that is what was destroyed when 'you' colonized them. It was the group that was real, not the lone individual. Thus, to portray one man as representing the group is an example of white bias."

"Okay. So you're supposed to put the white guy on one side and a tribe of Indians on the other?"

"Tribe is not the right word either. That's another thing we get wrong, according to him. When we white folks think of Indians we think of the Sioux, or people like them: horse-riding, tepee-living, buffalo-hunting natives of the great plains. Around here, according to him, most native people existed as small family bands. Extended families, groups of ten-twenty people."

"So, what are you going to do?"

Turghoff shook his head. He had a flash of himself a few hours earlier, alone in his studio. It is night. The world is silent. The canvas is before him, a brush in his hand. The feel of the brush, the smell of the room, his feet solid on the floor, his weight balanced. Nothing exists in that moment but the canvas, the brush, the array of colors on his palette and the impulse to create, a pure, true impulse to bring a form, a shape, a color, a pattern, to deliver it from his imagination into this hard, imperfect, chaotic, static-filled world of physical objects. *That impulse is who I am,* he told himself now. *That is why I am here. Everything else is just clutter.*

"I don't know," he said to her. "I want to do the mural as it is. I like the design, the mood, the dignity as I see it. But the problem is the folks at the tourist office. I could fudge a bit, just tell them that I talked to the native guy and he said the clothing looked okay to him. That's what they wanted me to find out."

Yvonne squirmed across from him, pushing against the back of the booth as she stretched her back, and he realized once again that as he revealed these thoughts to his pain-filled lover he was also confiding them to a reporter. So if he now went before the Tourist and Information Board and gave them an incomplete report would his "lover" feel she had to publish the complete story in the paper? Maybe interview the man at the university?

"The guy may just have been sparring with me for his own entertainment," Turghoff said as if to justify his proposed indiscretion. "I think he was enjoying himself. He had a glint in his eye the whole time. I finally asked: 'Well, is the design offensive? Should we not do the mural?'"

"And..?" Yvonne stretched her legs under the table, careful that she did not rub against his.

"And nothing. I could not get a straight answer out of the man. Just stories, jokes, parables. I got no yeses or noes. But on the drive back I began to think about the mural in a new way. Maybe using the image of a native man to welcome white people—that is, the descendants of those who conquered his people—to welcome them into what had been his land, is inherently insulting. He did not say that exactly but he may have been implying it. So, I'm going to have to think about it."

Yvonne was not listening. Her mind was clearly filled with discomfort..

"You look to be in pain," he said to her.

"That's very observant, Turghoff. But not a lot of help. I shouldn't have crouched like that."

"Anyway, to answer your question, I'm not one of those people who uses a regular doctor like for physicals and such. I try to stay away from them if I can."

"Okay."

"I did have this thing a couple of years ago. Here, on the index finger of my left hand. It had been there since I played baseball as a kid. I caught a lot of balls in my time and this thing grew there. For decades it never bothered me but then it started to swell and become sore. You hear about things like that becoming cancerous. So, I went to see old Doc Conrad at the clinic and he cut it out. It wasn't cancerous, as it turned out. I think he called it a cyst. That's my only recent experience with doctors. But Conrad has retired. He moved to Hawaii, I heard."

"Yeah, he's gone," she said, putting her purse on the table. "He was Florence's doc too."

"A few months ago I read in *The Woeful* about a new physician they hired at the clinic. A woman. Asian, I think. Chinese-American maybe. I gathered she doesn't actually live here. Doc Conrad lived here. He and his wife raised their kids here. This woman lives somewhere else. Drives down two or three days a week. Or maybe she flies in. Our vet has his own plane, did you know that? The guy I take Jocko to. He's not local either. He lives in Worley and flies back and forth, keeps an old car at the airstrip. The old vet used to live here..."

Turghoff paused seeing that Yvonne was busy digging in her purse.

But that is what was happening, he thought. Gradually, over time, more and more of our professionals have come to live somewhere else. Accountants, lawyers, even teachers commute. When he and Alicia first moved here, those professional people lived in town with their families. They cared about the schools, they attended PTA meetings. They joined the fire department, served on the chamber, the local sanitary board. That was no longer true and the town, his town, had come to feel hollowed out.

Yvonne pulled the white bottle from her purse and popped a pill into her mouth.

"That's the one," she said, swallowing. "Dr. Cheng. Ms. Sympathetic herself. God, does she do earnest and consoling, but it's all show. Some skit she learned in medical school and practices before a mirror. The bitch. Feeling no pain herself, she seems to think I am not feeling any either. You cannot believe how callous she is."

Robert Turghoff picked the check off the table. "Is she cutting you off cold turkey?"

"Might as well be. She wants to wean me, that's the term she used. As if I was sucking at her teat."

Turghoff closed his eyes. He took a deep breath. He knew he was making a mistake but he needed to say what he believed: "Maybe she's right, Yvonne. Maybe the door out of this is on the other side of the pain."

"Door out of what? A broken leg, crushed vertebrae?" Yvonne Curtiss sputtered these words in what seemed to him a shout. She slid to the end of the booth and pulled herself to her feet.

"Yvonne…"

"What can you possibly know about this? Do you feel what I feel? No way do you feel what I feel!"

"No…I…"

She grabbed the check from his hand and lurched toward the cash register. "And I can pay for my own damn coffee, thank you."

Turghoff sat with his arms on the table, hands enclosing the cooling cup. At the counter, the three men watched as Yvonne paid and then wrestled with the screeching door as she pushed herself out.

Hands in the pockets of her apron, Tanya stood at the cash register.

"What the hell got into her?" she asked Turghoff.

Robert Turghoff shrugged. "It's her back. She has a problem with her back." But it was not just that and he knew it.

CHAPTER THIRTY-ONE

Robert Turghoff stood on the sidewalk outside the Long Branch Café beneath the neon chef who continued to carefully flip his pancake. He had made a mistake; he knew that now. Who was he to offer advice? To think he could fix things? Did anyone or anything actually need to be fixed? It was politicians who fix the world, or claim to. Politicians who say they know what needs to be fixed. *You are not a politician. You are an artist damn it! An artist does not fix the world. An artist creates art.*

On the sidewalk a few yards away sat the man with his dog and his Styrofoam cup faithfully waiting just where his Mama had allegedly told him to wait. As Turghoff watched, the man removed a pouch of tobacco and some papers from his shirt and rolled himself a cigarette.

When Alicia and he first arrived in town there were no people sitting on sidewalks begging for change. No clusters of mentally challenged drug users camping in the weedy corners of vacant lots. But was it better back then? In those days ancient forests were being destroyed; loggers and hippies were caught in a bitter fight over the future of Big Hill, particularly the remaining old growth on the north and easterly sides. People regularly got into brawls in the local bars and drove home reckless and drunk. Was that better? Does anything ever really get better?

Down the sidewalk from his right came now an old man pushing a bicycle. The handlebars and bike's frame were so weighted down with filthy nylon and plastic bags that it seemed to Turghoff the contraption could never be ridden. The man was tall, gaunt, hook-nosed, his face dark from weather and grime, his grayish hair greasy, uncut and uncombed. He wore a tattered ill-fitting herringbone-tweed sport coat over a gray T-shirt above brown baggy slacks that were torn and unraveling around his decrepit shoes.

"This is the third novel this guy has stuck me in and I'm sick of it," the old man said, pausing his walk.

Is he speaking to me or just muttering to himself? Turghoff had no idea. But he felt obliged to respond. "What?" he asked.

The man removed a filthy hand from the bicycle and extended it palm up toward Turghoff. From a pocket in his shorts Turghoff removed the last of his change, a quarter and a dime which he placed in the man's hand.

"First it was Chicago, then San Francisco," the man muttered as he moved on. "And now he's got me walking through this wasteland."

Turghoff watched the man roll the bicycle away. When he turned, the fellow on the sidewalk was taking the last drag off his cigarette. The dog moved about at the end of its cord sniffing everything within reach of its nose.

The door squawked as he reentered the café. He felt weak, unsteady on his feet. He placed his hands on the counter and leaned across toward the waitress.

"Tanya, can I have a bowl of water?"

"A what?" She was looking at him strangely.

"There's a dog outside. I want to give it some water."

"Aw!" Tanya used the tone of voice some people employ when they want to express pity without really feeling it. "Like a cereal bowl or something?"

"Yes, like that."

She shook her head. "Sorry. We're short already. I sometimes have to serve oatmeal in chipped bowls. Like around eight when the place fills up we're using every bowl we got. If the boss saw a dog on the sidewalk drinking from one of our bowls…"

"Something," Turghoff heard himself pleading. "Anything that holds water. A takeout box maybe."

"A takeout box of water?"

"Yes, exactly!"

The three men still sitting at the end of the counter were paying close attention to the conversation and when Tanya had filled a takeout box with water and was cautiously handing it across the counter, one of them said: "You start with that, Turghoff, and you know what's gonna happen."

A second man nodded. "That dog's as hungry as he is thirsty."

"Yep, there'll be no end to it," the first man agreed.

Laughing, the third man said, "Yeah, Tanya. Tell Luis back there to fry up a steak for the dog."

"Make that a chicken-fried, Luis!" the first man shouted toward the kitchen.

The men were still guffawing as Turghoff pushed his way through the squawking door with his dripping box of water.

Back on the sidewalk he found that the man and dog had disappeared. He looked both ways down the street but saw no sign of either. What he did notice was a boy of six or seven in a blue shirt riding an orange bike, wearing an orange helmet and making graceful sweeps and turns along the sidewalk ahead of a tall blonde with a ponytail who followed the boy with two well-groomed poodles on leashes. One white, one black.

Standard French poodles, trimmed and set out and doing their prance and the boy on his bike and the woman wearing a white quilted vest over a blue turtleneck. The color of the turtleneck seemed to match perfectly the boy's shirt. The image brought Alicia, his Bostonian first wife into Turghoff's mind. Alicia had loved standard-sized French poodles. Albert,

Alicia's black poodle, referencing Camus, had predated their marriage and survived their divorce.

From the forgotten box, drops of water splashed onto Turghoff's sandalled foot. Alicia, he now realized, had looked (and certainly felt) as foreign and as ill-placed in this town as the woman approaching him must feel. Into this belated revelation, Howard Piggott suddenly arrived from behind him, a cavalry captain in full command of his high-powered wheelchair. Turghoff felt a shift of displaced air as the man brought his machine to an abrupt halt.

"Turghoff!" Piggott announced in his bold voice. "Just the man I want to see."

Turghoff felt a spasm in one of the muscles running up his back; it was as if he had been wrestling with Headlong Montoya. He glanced at the dripping box, and having no idea what to do with it, moved it farther away from his body.

"Howard," he said looking down on the man's salty red hair.

"About that mural, Turghoff. I received a telephone call yesterday from Clarence Wyckoff. Do you remember Clarence?"

Turghoff had no memory of Clarence Wyckoff.

"Used to manage the local office of the phone company before they broke it up and sent everyone packing. President of Rotary one year. Did a stint on the chamber. Got drunk and spilled his glass of red wine all over my wife's white dress one night while he was flirting with her at a fundraiser for the clinic."

Turghoff shook his head. Nearly empty now, the soggy box had stopped dripping.

"The phone company used to provide ten-fifteen good high-paying jobs in this town. Operators, linemen, management staff. All gone now. Just a few autonomous machines left humming away in an empty building. Like the story about the company that had two employees. You heard that one?"

Turghoff shook his head again.

"Two employees, one man and one dog," Howard Piggott continued, grinning a sly grin. "The man's job was to feed the dog, and the dog's job was to keep the man away from the machinery." Story told, Howard laughed happily.

"You said something about the mural?"

"Clarence Wyckoff is with the family."

"What family?"

"The family that owns the building, son."

"Oh, the toy store," Turghoff said. "With the wall, where we want to do the mural."

"Now you're clicking. And a fractious family it is. Clarence tells me they would likely not agree if the sun was up or down if they were meeting outside at noon. But emails have been flying back and forth and he wanted to hear from the local end so he called me."

They both watched as the boy with the orange helmet riding the orange bike did two circles around them with a serious expression on his face, and his mother walked past with a condescending smile, and the black poodle aimed a sniff at the useless box Turghoff held in his hand.

"Okay," Robert Turghoff said.

"They are not totally opposed and I did what I could to encourage the idea, Turghoff."

"Thank you, Howard."

"According to Wyckoff they are leaning toward the idea of a mural but they are going to require a small change."

"Excuse me a second, Howard." Turghoff walked to the curb and dropped the box into the gutter and returned to Howard Piggott.

"Takeout?"

"Not exactly. So, a small change you say?"

"No one in the family lives here anymore. Wyckoff was the last one and he's somewhere south of the Bay Area now."

"Okay."

"But they still own the damn building. An ancestor built it, you know, and had it moved from down by the river to its present location after the floods. That was well before both our times, Turghoff."

"Okay," Turghoff said yet again.

"So, they seem to think they own not just the building but the town, having a blood relative who started it. We're dealing with a group mind here, Turghoff, and a group mind is a dangerous thing."

"A small change?" Robert Turghoff asked again, grimacing.

"To get a consensus, son. A fractious group, as I said. There was a lot of argument about the Indian of course. Wyckoff says they finally got past the Indian but got stuck on the white guy. All emails flying around you understand. No phone calls, no actual meeting. These people do not come face to face if they can help it."

"The early settler?"

"The fellow looks too much like a frontiersman according to Wyckoff. Their ancestor was not a frontiersman. He was a merchant, a businessman. It was businessmen who built this town, not some guy with a rifle and a Bowie knife stuck in his belt. The family is clear on that."

"But the mural is not intended to show the actual gentleman…"

"I know what you're saying, Turghoff. I hear it loud and clear. But then it is not my building or my ancestor. My people came down from Oregon with the timber boom after the war. These people got here long before that."

"A businessman…"

"Now you're hearing me. A businessman standing behind a counter. That's what the family is thinking. Wyckoff likes the idea of a cat curled up on the counter but that is just his personal preference. From what I understand the family is not insisting on the cat. Myself, I see a potbelly stove in the corner, a cracker barrel or two in front. Some shelves of inventory visible behind the man would be a nice touch: stacks of linens, a few eggs in one of those wire baskets, you know the kind, a jar of horehound candy…." Howard Piggott paused to take a deep breath. "But you're the artist, not me."

"They're insisting…?" Turghoff said.

"Wyckoff would be happy to see the Indian airbrushed off the wall entirely. He told me that straight away. His ancestors lost cattle to the few Indians left around here. But apparently the family as a whole has accepted the Indian though it would look a little silly, don't you think, him standing there in the forest like some noble savage with the store opposite. Maybe he can be shown coming through the door looking for a plug of tobacco, or bringing in a mess of fish to sell. Something like that. The Indian as customer, keeping with the theme you might say."

"I'll have to think about it," Robert Turghoff said, trying to stretch his back.

"You do that. Get those creative juices flowing. Fractious, like I said. A fractious family."

With that Howard Piggott sped away. Robert Turghoff looked first one way down the street and then the other. No sign of the man with the sign and the dog. Apparently his Mama had given him new instructions.

CHAPTER THIRTY-TWO

Over the next three weeks as autumn deepened there appeared in *The Woeful*, beneath the byline of Yvonne Curtiss, three articles on the homeless population in and around Long Branch. Turghoff found them stunning. Deep in the forest on the north side of Big Hill she had crawled inside a giant hollowed-out redwood stump to speak with an isolate huddled there, a man whose only desire, it seemed, was to cower as far from society as possible. She explored camps under bridges and in clearings hidden inside patches of dense underbrush that were accessible only through broken wire fencing. She counted occupants and interviewed those who would communicate. She described a rudimentary subculture in one camp dominated by a tattooed ex-con whom she characterized as macho, charismatic and deranged.

In one patch of weeds she discovered a gold-painted, cast-iron frame from a grand piano that must have weighed four hundred pounds and had to have been dragged a mile or more before being abandoned. She photographed syringes, needles, feces. She described sprawls of broken bicycles and shopping carts, mounds of abandoned clothing, discarded sleeping bags and backpacks sprawled on trampled ground sprinkled with tossed-aside, still-colorful logo-flashing plastic and paper packaging. It was, she wrote, as if an overnight flurry had fallen from the sky, but what settled on the earth had not been frozen water, but refuse from America's marketing dreams.

The articles amazed Robert Turghoff. They were dynamic, rich with detail and color. And it was not just the articles themselves; engaged readers began filling *The Woeful* with letters in response. He could think of little but Yvonne Curtiss. He wanted to applaud her work. He wanted to talk with her about the mural disaster which had him enraged. (A band of natives? A shopkeeper behind a counter! Who did they think he was? Some "Show me your swatches, Ma'am" by-the-hour housepainter?) He wanted to hold her, catch her scent, listen to her, make love to her. But Yvonne Curtiss ignored and avoided him at every turn. No visits to his place. No chance encounters on the street. No mention of the mural in the paper. His calls and emails were not returned.

One afternoon, he suspected, she managed to escape through the back door of *The Woeful* office just as he entered the front, leaving him to face a stammering Mel Kline and then his mother Florence, who soon emerged from a back office. It had been several years since Turghoff had caught more than a distant glimpse of Florence Kline. Her person had shrunk; her face had aged dramatically but her hair remained as black as it had been the year he and Alicia arrived. The contrast seemed to somehow highlight the aging of her body and face.

"No, but thank you for inquiring," Florence said to him. "We will certainly tell her you stopped by."

§

Carly came past the house one afternoon each of the first two weeks. He left her alone to work in the studio, but something had changed it seemed to him. She wore black now, and instead of walking she arrived on a silver push scooter with red fenders that she hoisted up on her shoulder when she reached the gravel drive.

Perhaps puberty had struck, or fashion: acne now speckled her forehead, her jeans had rips just above the knees; the elongated sleeves of her pullovers left only her fingers exposed. It struck Turghoff in those moments that the contours of her face were coming to more resemble those of her mother but he could not trust this observation. He was too emotionally invested and he knew it.

Both times before she left, she brought her sketchbook into the house and showed it to him. She had worked on sketches of Jocko and of the plants he had set up for his own work. He liked the way her drawings were becoming looser, more open and flowing and he told her so. Of her mother she said nothing unless asked, and then only that she was very busy, seldom home, and when home, bent over her computer or examining photos on her phone. Turghoff was hesitant to ask at all but could not resist and then felt clammy and defeated after.

The third time Carly came, Turghoff saw through the kitchen window that she was leaving without saying goodbye. He rushed to the door and asked her to come in.

"I want to see your work."

"I'm embarrassed," she told him.

"Be brave," he said, leading her into the house.

They sat side by side on the sofa; she with her backpack on her lap.

Carly looked reluctant, almost petulant, but after some hesitation she finally unzipped the pack. She had begun to comb her dark hair down over her forehead in a failed attempt to hide the emerging acne. As she wrested the sketchbook free from the pack, he recognized the first suggestion of breasts swelling beneath her turtleneck. He turned abruptly away, looking toward the window where the plum tree was visible in the yard with its lovely yellowing leaves.

When she had finished flipping the pages up and over the spiral top, she said, "So."

Turghoff turned back and found himself staring at a precise copy of his own portrait of her mother. It was not a full copy. It provided no rendition of the feet and ankles that had so intrigued him that first day. She had framed the drawing from the enlarged key at her waist to the crown of her mother's head; the hair, he realized, was subtly different from his sketch, more vibrant, more on the edge of disarray.

For a long time the two of them looked in silence at the drawing. Finally Turghoff admitted to himself and to her: "You fixed the nose."

And Carly Curtiss nodded, pleased with herself.

CHAPTER THIRTY-THREE

The pleasure Robert Turghoff took in his own work suffered horribly during this period. After bracing himself with late morning coffee followed by two eggs, carefully turned in bacon grease, and two pieces of well-buttered toast, he was able to function normally through the day. He worked in the garden, delivered prints to the post office; he shopped and chatted with those he met.

If it was over, he told himself, it was over. It had to end sometime. He knew that and so did she. He would forget about the stupid mural, forget about her and get on with his life and work.

But at night in the studio his resolve failed him. He had begun an ambitious painting shortly before the disastrous confrontation in the café. It was a large canvas that he was filling with images of teasels. Autumn teasel flowerheads, that most beautiful of natural objects. The idea was density: pack them in, present their astonishing shapes from different distances and angles; show the spiny leaves, the thorny stalks, the fuzzy heads with their wildly curling bracts. He wanted teasels on top of teasels, one or two with their remaining lavender-flower fringes surrounding them like tutus. But dense, clustered, a rich compression of varying browns broken by small flashes of lavender fleurettes. He wanted precision and detail, detail upon detail.

The first couple of nights he had rushed from his bed to get back to the work. But now when he switched on the array of carefully positioned lights and approached the canvas, he felt only trepidation. This was the most precious time of his twenty-four-hour day, the few hours when he was most awake, most truly himself, but he could no longer trust his impulses.

A disturbing vacancy filled the studio. Yvonne's absence was everywhere and would not let him go. Each teasel he attempted to add to the canvas caused an internal struggle. The channel extending from mind to hand felt clotted and confused. His brush wanted to distort the lovely form and structure of an object that—it had always seemed to him—was already perfect and could not be improved upon. His impulse now was to disfigure: to stretch and compress, to twist and discolor. One night, in a wild passion, he filled the entire canvas with fragments, with slivers and chunks of teasel matter. The images were distorted, extended, shrunken, painted in discordant colors and harshly conjoined.

When the dawn finally came, he felt as if he were awaking from a trance or dream. As he cleaned his brushes and studied the canvas he thought he might have created something new, something original and of lasting value. But the next night when he returned to the studio and turned on the lights, he realized that the painting was a disaster, ugly, monstrous, and in some obscure way, obscene, an embarrassment he felt compelled to destroy. Fortunately, he had used acrylic and the surface was dry. He quickly covered it over with a fresh layer of underpaint, followed by another, and then another.

Then one afternoon while he was stacking firewood, a NewFuel truck pulled off the road and came rumbling down the drive. He straightened himself and watched, surprised at how massive this blue object appeared when removed from the street and placed in his yard. Engine churning it pushed through the lower branches of the plum shredding leaves and twigs. Its heavy tires crushed and spit rocks as it turned and backed toward the green propane tank. When the hulking beast finally stopped and fell silent, Gil Curtiss climbed from the cab. The cuffs of his blue NewFuel shirt were turned up to just below the elbows and he stood legs apart as he pushed his hands into a pair of dark work gloves.

Gil Curtiss was a large man Turghoff realized once again, a head taller than himself with strong shoulders, a thick torso and trunk-like legs. It would be short and brutal, should it come to that; Gil Curtiss would transform him into mash. But he also saw something uncertain and fumbling about the man as he pulled free the hose and approached the tank. Uncomfortable, or maybe a haze of loss surrounded him.

They greeted one another cautiously, Curtiss removing his right glove to shake and then pulling it back on as Turghoff, nodding, stepped back a stride. He was eager to ask about Yvonne and he assumed Curtiss was resisting the urge to approach the same subject. But neither was prepared to discuss that which was central to them, so they had little to talk about beyond passing mention of Carly's drawings, the weather, the price of propane, the splitting and stacking of firewood, the mechanics and challenges of driving a large truck filled with fuel.

"Yeah," Turghoff said wearily, when the exchange finally sputtered and died.

"Right."

There was no wind and no traffic on the road; the afternoon was cool and quiet, the air smelled of propane. When the tank had been filled and the hose was again locked securely on the rear of the truck, Gil Curtiss removed his gloves and held them in his large hand. He took a deep breath and scanned the yard.

"I was sort of hoping to find her here," he said.

"Carly?" Turghoff asked, surprised.

"No, Vonnie."

"Ah…" Turghoff was not prepared to explore all the implications of that remark, but one was obvious: they were two men, both of whom were worried about, obsessed by, and in love with the same woman.

They stood very still, looking away from each other. Piled high with firewood, the rusty wheelbarrow stood balanced and stout where he had left it midway between the splitter and lean-to outside his kitchen door.

"I haven't seen her in three weeks," Turghoff said. "I think I ruined our…our friendship. About the pills. I spoke to her about the pills."

"Ahh." Curtiss nodded.

"I decided there was a problem with the pills. But it was my mistake, my intrusion, and I regret it. What do I know about how anyone should manage their life?"

Gil Curtiss nodded again. "There is a problem. With the pills, but yeah."

"It's hard enough just managing my own."

"Yeah," Gil Curtiss said again. "It might have nothing to do with you. She's all the time at the camps now. Everyday. Writing, photographing. She thinks there's a book in it. About 'living rough' and the town. Two different worlds sharing the same space. That's what she's doing."

"Alone?" Turghoff wanted to know.

"So far as I know."

CHAPTER THIRTY-FOUR

A few days later it rained overnight, the first real rain since spring. Working in the studio that night, Turghoff heard it arrive, a gentle tapping on the skylights that for a moment alarmed him. Then it turned to steady pounding, and the sound was so familiar it seemed it had never really been absent. A sense of relief accompanied the rain; Long Branch had survived another summer without serious fire.

After the usual late breakfast, Turghoff checked his email account and found the long-awaited letter from the attorney in San Francisco. The family, she was pleased to report, had reached a consensus regarding the mural. While his offer to resurface the wall was appreciated and acceptable to the family, the mural image as presented was not.

The attorney proposed that he redesign the mural and resubmit it for the family's consideration. While she could not guarantee that a revised image would be approved, a mural that featured the likeness of the family's ancestor, and the town's founder, would be the one most likely to succeed. She kindly attached a photograph of the gentleman himself. The black and white image, which seemed to possess a vaguely rose-colored tint, depicted a stern mustachioed fellow with dark hair and suit seated in a stuffed chair with his legs apart, hands on his thighs. A watch fob hung from his vest, a white handkerchief protruded from the breast pocket of his coat and a dutiful wife stood beside the chair in a full-length, rather elegant dress that featured dramatically puffed shoulders. It struck him as odd that the two long-dead individuals were a decade or more younger than he was.

After he had read the email and studied the photograph, Turghoff thought of Yvonne. How would she react, were she here? Would they laugh together or would they cry? Would she imagine herself in that woman's lovely dress? He did.

In the afternoon he decided to hike the trails carved along the flanks of Big Hill. Though he lived alone, he needed to leave the familiar at times to find solitude and this was particularly true now. The rain had ended before he parked Old Ugly at the trailhead. When he stepped out of the truck and slammed the door, the damp air smelled alive, fresh and real.

The potent air reminded him of the sourdough starter Jen had kept in a crock on the kitchen counter. Early mornings he liked to sneak in, lift the ceramic lid and take a good whiff. Jen was not happy about this practice. She feared some part of him, perhaps a hair from his head or unruly mustache, might fall into the broth. Jen had been as protective of her sourdough starter as Solomon was of his wine must. Back in the days when his house had a family in it.

The dirt path with redwoods towering above and graceful, nodding sword ferns below was strewn with sprigs of rust-red needles. The trees dripped and the moist earth cushioned the fall of his boots. He needed the exertion of elevation gain and the focus demanded by uneven, root-infested, switchbacking single-track. He had no desire to think or plan or decide; he wanted to move beyond thought and image to clarity.

He hiked for over an hour and when he reached the top and stepped onto the graveled edge of the parking area where he and Yvonne had once surveyed the town, he saw an elderly couple standing beside a white Toyota sedan. They wore matching blue and white windbreakers and white hats and they stood with their arms around each other admiring the view. The image was so charming, so intimate that he felt himself an invader, and before they noticed him, he turned back into the trees.

He was descending, enjoying the quiet and feeling the bounce that comes from having completed hard work when he came upon his friend Solomon. Seated upon a green metal bench that overlooked a canyon, Solomon looked decidedly unbouncy.

Sometimes in the forest, people wanted to be alone. Turghoff himself had wanted to be alone. When he met someone on the trail, even someone he knew, he had only nodded and quickly moved on. But here sat Solomon, alone and perhaps disconsolate.

Turghoff sat down on the bench and looked out over the deep wooded canyon and said nothing.

After some time Solomon tapped the plaque on the back of the bench. "Did you know this guy?"

Turghoff read the plaque which dedicated the bench to the memory of Theodore Edwards, MD. "I've heard of him," he said. "I don't know that I ever met him."

"He was the doc at the clinic before Conrad; Edwards started it actually. He retired before either you or I came on the scene. But I knew him because I did some work for him and his wife. The usual carpentry stuff around the house. His wife was in a wheelchair, polio I assume, and I built them a ramp or two."

"On Spruce Court?" Turghoff asked. "That white house at the end with the ramp and the tall trees behind it?"

"That's it. Interesting couple, a bit reclusive. But I talked to him a few times when I was thinking about changing careers. It was fun doing carpentry in my twenties but the idea of being sixty and doing it…. Anyway, I was attracted to medicine but it was too late to start down the road to an MD. Edwards suggested nursing or physician's assistant but I had a hankering for popping vertebrae."

"It has worked well for you, obviously…as Patty's assistant."

Solomon frowned. "Before you showed up I was thinking about something Edwards said to me years ago. I'd asked him what the worst thing was about practicing medicine."

"Let me guess. Checking some hairy dude's prostate?"

"Not close. The worst thing according to Edwards was patients who did not want to be cured."

"I don't get it."

"A guy comes in. He complains about his knees. His back is bothering him. He's overweight, he smokes constantly, he drinks to excess. His only exercise is punching the remote and opening and closing the refrigerator. He wants something for the pain he's experiencing. It's obvious what he needs. He needs to get off his ass, get over the cigarettes and the booze. Lose some weight, hike up here a couple days a week. But if you tell him that, first he won't do it and second he'll hate you for pointing it out. 'Just give me something for the pain,' that's all he can say. Edwards told me that was the worst. Trying to help people who didn't really want to be helped."

Down in the canyon they saw a couple following an unleashed black and tan dog along a trail; the woman following the dog was followed a few steps behind by the man. As they approached a small footbridge the dog jumped off the trail and began to drink from the creek. The couple stopped on the bridge. They leaned over the railing watching the dog and the woman removed a blue bottle from the man's red pack. She took a swig and handed the bottle to the man. Then they started walking again and their voices came up out of the canyon ordering the dog out of the water and back onto the trail.

"Edwards said that for patients like that, the problem they bring to you to fix, is actually their cure."

"What?"

"They won't admit that of course, not even to themselves. But what such a patient most wants is the problem he has, not its cure."

"I don't get it. If they want the problem why do they come in asking for a cure? That makes no sense to me."

"It does to me," Solomon said. "By the way, are you two still a thing?"

"Whaa…?" Robert Turghoff's body jerked, and he experienced a moment of intense confusion as if he were watching a kaleidoscope spinning before his eyes. But then the pieces slowed and settled into a pattern. He glanced at Solomon who seemed focused on the huge burnt-out redwood stump that stood to their immediate left.

"Tell me," Turghoff asked his friend, "as a chiropractor can you write prescriptions?"

"I cannot," Solomon said. "And if I could I would not. I manage my patients inside other parameters. If I believed my patient really required medication I would recommend they see a physician. But what I will not ever do is ring up a doctor and tell him or her that in my opinion 'our patient' needs pain medication. That I will not do."

"I take it you've been asked to do that."

"I can't talk about it," Solomon said. He stood and walked to the edge of the canyon where beneath a small patch of open sky a few asters were blooming.

The two men admired the lavender asters with their gold buttons, and they looked down into the canyon where the trees rose straight and tall beside their dead, down and slowly decaying ancestors. A raven spoke and its voice entered and filled the canyon and then the sound disappeared. The trees rose up through deep shade and the slanting yellow shafts of sunlight, and it felt to Turghoff at that moment that the canyon was a huge bowl filled to its brim with silence, a profound, peace-filled silence.

Moments later they began walking together down the trail. At their vehicles, Turghoff invited Solomon to join him for a Cubano at the Trailhead Pub. He was not ready as yet to return to an empty house. But Solomon declined.

"Have you taken a good look at the wine list in that place?"

"I was thinking of an IPA."

"'Will you have the red with that, sir, or the white?' Besides, I have a Parcheesi date. Carly is staying over with Britt, and Patty and I have committed ourselves to an evening with the high rollers."

CHAPTER THIRTY-FIVE

In the Trailhead Pub Turghoff sat at the bar with his sandwich and his mug of beer and the sound system blasted beat-heavy music, presumably to keep the staff hustling. A huge screen on the wall behind the bar showed scenes from what appeared to be a triathlon taking place somewhere with palm trees. Because the TV sound was muted his impressions were muddled: a mob of men swimming toward a yellow buoy, then turning and swimming back to land and then running up the beach toward bicycles. Then a mob of women swimming and the men cycling through tight curves; then the women running to their bicycles and the men jumping off their bikes and chasing one another along a track. Then a woman crashing her bike and people rushing to help her. The cumulative effect made Turghoff realize that the exercise he had accomplished that afternoon on Big Hill had been rather insignificant.

On a second screen, adjacent to the first, a woman was interviewing a man in a baseball uniform. Their lips moved but no sound came through the speakers. Their body language, however, suggested a complex narrative.

At that point Jim Franklin, the old logger wearing a bright MAGA hat, sat down on the stool next to him.

"Turghoff, how's your back?"

For good measure Franklin placed a slap on Turghoff's shoulder blades.

"My back's okay, Jim. How's yours?"

Turghoff had no idea why Franklin was interested in his back but he resisted the temptation to return the slap. At that point Manny the bartender came up and asked Franklin what he wanted.

"Before I tell you, answer me this."

"What's that?"

"What's your most expensive scotch?"

"Macallan 25. You want a shot?"

"What would it cost me?"

"Seventy-five a shot," Manny said. "You interested?"

"I'll settle for a beer, but I have a story for you."

"Okay," Manny said, glancing at Turghoff.

"Man walks into a bar. He tells the bartender he wants twelve shots of Macallan 25 and he wants them set out in a row in front of him, twelve single shots."

"Okay."

"So the bartender sets up the row of shot glasses and carefully pours out the booze."

Manny nods.

"The man picks up the first shot glass and slugs it down. Then he grabs the second glass and slugs that down."

"Okay." Manny glanced again at Turghoff.

"The bartender's watching this real close and after the third shot, he says to the fellow, 'That stuff is pretty expensive, friend. You might want to savor it a little.'"

"All right."

"But the man keeps right on. He grabs the fourth glass and the fifth and slugs them down and then he says, 'If you had what I got you'd slug 'em down too.'"

"Okay," Manny says.

"The bartender feels a little guilty as he watches the man slug down the sixth and seventh shots so he says, 'I'm sorry to hear that, friend, what is it that you got?'

"The man grabs the eighth shot glass. He slugs it down and as he reaches for the ninth, he says to the bartender, 'One dollar.'"

Manny studied Jim Franklin for a moment and then he said, "What kind of beer do you want?"

"I'll take what he's having," Franklin said, nodding toward Turghoff.

When Manny had left Franklin said to Turghoff, "I saw you going into Solomon's the other day. From the way you moved, I figured it was your back."

"The other day?"

To Turghoff it seemed as though his visit to Solomon's had happened a lifetime ago. Up on the screen the woman who had crashed her bike was standing before a red backdrop talking into a microphone. The sound was still muted and Turghoff could not hear a word she was saying.

CHAPTER THIRTY-SIX

It was nearing dark when Turghoff finally returned to his house, and the air rushing through the open window of the clattering truck was damp and noticeably cooler than before. The uneven gravel driveway caused the headlights on Old Ugly to send out bouncing shafts of light that first illuminated objects and then hid them, and at first he did not recognize what a moment later filled him with sudden joy: parked shyly against the side of the studio was Yvonne's midnight-blue Mazda convertible, the top up, the windows closed, the interior empty.

He gasped. So real it was, so *there*. For an instant he imagined he smelled an aroma permeating the interior of that car, something she wore or used, a perfume, a shampoo, a skin cream, and the whiff of it filled him with longing.

He felt mischievous suddenly, sneaky as he cut the lights and killed the engine. She would be in the spa waiting for him. Perhaps she had the jets on and had not heard his arrival. He stepped from the truck and carefully closed the door. It was deathly silent and dark beneath the plum where he had parked. Before him stood every feature of his home and life, clear, precise and gray-tinted in the fading light: his house, his studio, the fenced pool and garden, the upper branches of the apple tree and the pear that he and Jen had planted a decade before. The branches showed in black silhouette against dusky gray clouds on the horizon and the translucent blue sky above. How still it was.

He entered the dark house stealthily, closing the door behind him. Standing in the entrance he removed his boots and socks; he stripped off his vest, his shirt and his shorts, heavy with keys, change, wallet and pocketknife, and then he dropped his undershorts to the floor. *Do you paint in the nude?* she had asked him that first day. He felt himself a kid again and had to stifle a giggle. Then he recognized her own clothing tossed recklessly on the couch. Had she been hoping to surprise him?

Access to the spa was through a door on the far side of his bedroom. Robert Turghoff entered this innermost sanctum of his home. When he reached the door, he paused. Yes, the jets were on. Grinning, he turned the handle and dramatically pulled open the door.

It was dark, the objects indistinct, the jets rumbling. But he could make out Yvonne. She was seated in the spa across from him as if awaiting his arrival. Except her face was not directed toward him. The dim oval form he was seeing, he realized, was not her face but the pale white of her rounded back. Her face and head appeared to be submerged in the churning water.

When she failed to move, Turghoff ran. He leaped over the near side of the spa and into the hot water, his knees banging against the floor, his own head plunging for a moment beneath the surface. Gasping, he gripped her shoulders and pushed up and back, lifting her head and shoulders up out of the water and shoving her against the seat back.

Her face was now in the open air, but she did not gasp or cough as he expected, and for a second this astonished him. He felt as if he was doing something wrong, as if there were some switch or mechanism he needed to activate to awaken her. But she did not awaken. Her features were very pale and her lips bluish, almost purple; her head lolled to one side, her dead weight pressed heavily against his hands and arms.

CPR! He knew this. Years before he had volunteered for the fire department. He and Alicia had taken the course in a backroom of the clinic, he a couple of times. Get her onto her back. Push her head back, force open her mouth and clear her throat. Press your hands against her chest. Breathe into her mouth, get into a rhythm.

But first he had to get her out of the water. Jesus! His every effort to push her up onto the rim of the spa failed. His knees and feet were slipping on the spa floor and when he paused to regain his balance she would again fall forward into the water.

How astonishingly heavy she was! After several minutes he managed to center himself squat-like in the water while pushing her up toward the rim. Finally he had her balanced against the outer edge. He managed to turn her so her feet were also free of the water, but she continued to lean precariously toward him. He had to get her out of the spa and onto the floor without dropping her. Continually gasping for air, he slid his left arm under her back and his right under her thighs and with all his strength he attempted to push her up and over the seatback as the jets rumbled and the water churned and the heat rising from the spa threatened to suffocate him.

Twice he heaved and each time he slipped and fell forward, and she dropped back into the water and onto the seat where he landed clumsily on top of her. Finally after much struggle he got his knees onto the seat and with her in his arms, he managed to lift, balancing her precariously on the rim. But he could not hold her there, and she fell heavily out of the spa and onto the floor. *My God, I am beating her to death!*

Turghoff climbed from the spa and knelt beside the body spread awkwardly on the wooden floor, the boards of which decades before he had milled and planed and hammered into place. How detailed their dim outline appeared to him at that moment.

He was pressing rhythmically against her chest now with both hands. Then he was holding her face and breathing air into her mouth. He performed these motions for what seemed like forever until he finally realized that he was passionately kissing her passive lips. He was kissing her and forcing his tongue into her unresponsive mouth as if they were in an orgasmic embrace, or at least he was.

It was as if he thought his love could bring her back. If she could be made to feel again what he felt for her, his desire would entice her to return. But she did not return. Yvonne Curtiss was dead. Gone. The object lying clumsily on the floor beside him was a corpse. Human flesh from which the human had departed. In the darkening spa Robert Turghoff began to sob.

CHAPTER THIRTY-SEVEN

How long he sobbed, how long he knelt on the hard floor, his body hunched over hers he would never be able to say; perhaps for a short while he dozed. At some point he or the machinery must have turned off the jets because a great silence surrounded him. Not simply silence, he felt himself in the presence of an all-encompassing absence.

It had become fully dark. Only the faint light from a scattering of distant stars illuminated her form and his own. He touched her face and then drew his hand back in horror. Her passive body had already begun to cool and this struck him as a hideous offense against nature. He thought to lift her back into the hot water but the terror he had experienced getting her out had been so overwhelming he could not do it.

He too was cold. He found robes on a bench. He wrapped one around himself and taking another knelt again beside her pale form. The body, whose movements had always exemplified a natural grace, struck him now as uniquely awkward, as clumsy, as abandoned. Yes, abandoned.

He placed a ratty blue towel over her feet and with the white terrycloth robe he covered everything but her face and throat. He had no idea what the time was but he knew he should call someone. 9-1-1? The sheriff's substation? Gil? But he had no number for Gil.

He stood again. He went to the switch beside the bedroom door and flipped on the wall lights that illuminated the spa; for a moment the intense light caused him to cover his eyes. Then, when he could see again, how familiar the space looked and how incongruous was her body spread on the floor.

Then he noticed the candles. Yvonne had brought several candles and set them up along the benches that lined the walls. She had always said he should keep candles in the spa and this time she had brought them. She had planned it out, he realized. She had prepared herself and had come to be with him.

He saw her familiar black purse lying on a bench next to one of the candles. He approached and beside the purse he found a small box of wooden matches and next to the matches half-hidden beneath the purse was an empty syringe with a needle protruding from the end.

Turghoff gasped. The needle explained everything.

"You whore!" he shouted. "You fucking bitch! That's what sent you to the camps. A book my ass! You went in search of drugs."

He grabbed the syringe and hurled it at her body. The syringe struck the floor with a timid plasticky sound; it skittered across the room and came to rest in the shadow beneath a bench as if it had fled eager to hide itself from the world.

Turghoff turned the lights off. He stood panting in the darkened space, and as he stood there her pain and desperation engulfed him. He felt it keenly and personally as if it were his pain, his desperation.

"I'm sorry!" he cried. "I am so sorry!"

Stumbling and almost falling he ran and knelt beside her body. Sobbing, he stretched himself out and lay beside and on top of her.

You are free of it now, dear girl: the broken bones, the crushed vertebrae, the rotten teeth, the pain. All of it. You are free now of all the pain; you have left it here with me.

And stroking her hair, he continued to sob.

§

A short time later he sat up telling himself again that he must call someone. A death had occurred here. He had a responsibility. Someone had to be informed. Then he pictured Patty and Solomon, Britt and Carly; they sat at a card table playing Parcheesi. The innocence of that image stunned him.

The thing about Parcheesi was that it was all about innocence, he realized. Who won and who lost resulted from pure chance. It had nothing to do with skill or blame, with honors earned or mistakes made. You followed the rules, you rolled the dice and the random numbers told you what to do. How wonderful that seemed to him just then. Life as pure chance, as pure luck with no credit and no guilt. No blame, no shame.

The image held vivid in his mind: the card table and the four of them gathered around it. Secure to Patty's left is a bowl of popcorn; he could smell the warm butter. In Solomon's hand a small delicate glass contains a fluid expensive and dark. He watches Carly take up the canister, and making that little frown so familiar when she was drawing, she shakes the canister and rolls out the dice.

And the dice announce that her mother is dead.

Except they do not! And that was the revelation that suddenly struck him. At that card table at that moment, Yvonne Curtiss was alive. To Carly, her mother was alive. She was alive to Britt, to her friend Patty and to Solomon her chiropractor. Around the entire world, everywhere except within the confines of this spa, Yvonne Curtiss was alive.

He watched Gil Curtiss stand up from the metal folding chair in the basement of the Lutheran church and heard him announce to the men and women seated in the oval around him: "My name is Gil Curtiss and I am an alcoholic." And as Gil Curtiss made that brave confession, his wife was alive.

To Florence and Mel Kline bickering or ignoring each other in their old two-story house beside the Catholic church— "The Incestuary" as she called it—their reporter Yvonne Curtiss was alive and on the job; Florence could stay pretty much retired and Mel could remain pretty much useless.

At a social event taking place that evening in Santa Rosa at the home of Yvonne's parents, as the caterers bustled about with drinks and canapés, as guests chatted, munched and drank, the hosts could be gracious and entertaining knowing that their daughter was alive. Difficult, troublesome—no, she had not turned out exactly as they had hoped—but she was alive.

Even the son of a bitch that Turghoff pictured beneath a blue tarp in some cluster of brush at the edge of town hunched over his ratty sleeping bag fingering a few crinkled dollar bills, even that bastard believed that his new paying customer was alive and would be back for more.

No, he, Robert Turghoff, would call no one. He had become the little Dutch boy who saved Haarlem by sticking his finger in the dike. Or his opposite. Rather than holding the ocean out, he would hold the grief in. Until the new day had fully arrived, he would hold back the grief. He would shoulder the full weight of it himself and with that modest gift Yvonne Curtiss could live through the night in the hearts of everyone who knew her. She would be alive everywhere in the world. Everywhere but here.

He got up. His fingers found the matchbox beside the purse and he walked around the spa and lit the seven candles she had carefully set out. Then he returned to her body and sat down beside her. The light from the candles flickered across their faces and the wrenching grief settled down and around him.

§

When daylight finally returned to the spa it was a gray light and it fell from a gray and indifferent sky. He snuffed out the three candles still burning and he took her phone from the purse and he placed a call.

"This is Robert Turghoff, Gil. I need you to come to my house. There is something I have to show you."

"Something?"

"Just come. And do not bring Carly."

He was standing at the front door when Gil Curtiss arrived. He watched Curtiss park his pickup beside the dark Miata that belonged to his wife. He parked it carefully, parallel to her car and adjacent as if he were fitting the pickup into a confined space. Curtiss emerged from the truck and approached the house, the sleeves of his blue NewFuel shirt rolled up, his skin a pleasing brown, and Turghoff saw before him a man whose large heart was sorely troubled and would soon be crushed. In some other world, he thought, he and this man might have become friends.

He led him through the living room past her garments folded now neatly on the couch and through the bedroom past the bed that had not been slept in and through the open door to the spa.

Gil Curtiss saw his wife's body stretched on the floor covered with a white robe and the syringe lying on the robe. His right hand rose to his throat. He fumbled with the leather strap, then he clasped the arrowhead and held it pressed against his chest.

Robert Turghoff said: "You are going to believe what you want to believe, or what you have to believe, but I will tell you all I know, as best and as honestly as I can."

CHAPTER THIRTY-EIGHT

04-15-2022
NAPLES

Elwood:

Sorry to hear that the Haut Gallery has closed. It was a fine space, intimate and well-lighted. Kitschy, eh? Well, if you say so. The show was titled Blackberry Winter. The "vegetative stuff" you refer to consisted of twenty-seven paintings that explored the transformation of the Himalayan blackberry as it passes through fall and into winter along the western coast of the US. I was struck first by the astonishing colors found in some few of its leaves, and the closer I looked, other aspects intrigued me as well. A teasel or two thrown in, a few ghostly stalks of finished hemlock and fennel, as I remember. I have found that death and decay in nature if rendered clearly and without sentimentality can be an intriguing and evocative subject. Perhaps it was Sergei's tragic death that set me on that path. Others have followed.

Fortunately all twenty-seven canvases found new homes. One of my most successful shows. Thus, I profited and the show helped David and Ben keep their lovely space open a while longer.

As to your diligent detective work, Elwood, there is one item that does not appear in your report: the identity of the young applicant. However, should her name be Carly Curtiss, I can assure you that she did indeed study in my studio and that at the age of twelve she did make an improved drawing of a drawing I had made of her mother. I have not seen her in several years so I cannot speak to her present work. But based on what I know of her skills and her character, her presence at the Institute will be of great benefit to the school and to the other students.

Yes, a Massachusetts state senator, and quite content so far as I know.

Caio, Turghoff

§

Robert Turghoff folded the letter and slipped it into an envelope. He sealed the envelope and placed it and the pen in his pouch. Beyond the table where he sat was a huge piazza crowded with people. Visible at the dock beyond the piazza a ferry and a white cruise ship (the first he had seen since the pandemic) were disgorging tourists, and beyond them were the blue waters of the bay.

A waiter approached with an espresso. Turghoff plucked the remaining caper off his plate and popped it into his mouth. Then he nodded and the waiter left the coffee and removed the wine glass, the utensils and empty plate.

The piazza was pedestrian only but as he watched a man in a white Fiat entered off a side street and was trying to drive through the crush of walkers. The driver was a handsome Italian, fifty or so, wearing a white shirt, a dark tie and suit. Slowly but persistently he nudged the vehicle forward as pedestrians stepped aside or hurried ahead. One young man refused to move. Standing firm he posed as a bullfighter waving an imaginary cape and shouting something Turghoff could not make out. The driver continued to inch ahead and the young man held himself steady and the approaching fender brushed against his jeans.

Of course she had used his name to enhance her application, he realized. Elwood had been right about that. At the funeral reception, pressed between her father and her grandmother, looking impossibly small and fragile, she had refused to look up when he offered his condolence, or to touch his extended hand even after her father nudged her.

She was the one he most betrayed, and her rejection had caused the deepest cut, deeper than Terry Clark's cold stare, or Solomon's shaking head, or the "I-told-you" expression frozen on Patty Solomon's distraught face. Maybe the words she wrote about his having been an inspiration were a calculated lie. He could accept that; news of her application delighted him. The impulse to create art had survived in Carly Curtiss, as it had in him.

He saw the white car, the well-attired driver, the colorful scrum of tourists and locals. Visible beyond the cruise ship was the Bay of Naples, its blue so intense it required him to squint. When he had finished the espresso and paid the bill Robert Turghoff stepped onto the piazza and soon disappeared in the crowd.

ACKNOWLEDGMENTS

I wish to express my thanks to the following individuals:
To Nina Haedrich for editing the manuscript, for emotional
support and for loving me.
To Bonnie Burgess for careful proofreading and comma and
semicolon diligence.
To Dennis Bourassa for advising me about the making of wine.
To Rip Kirby for the story Jim Franklin tells the bartender.
To Gordon Inkeles, on whose office door was a sign that
inspired the one Turghoff placed on his.

Doug Ingold is a native of Illinois. A retired lawyer and former Peace Corps Volunteer, he is the father of two adult children, a daughter and a son. He and his wife Nina Haedrich live on the Redwood Coast of northern California.

Visit dougingold.com

Milton Keynes UK
Ingram Content Group UK Ltd.
UKHW051411061024
449206UK00017B/140